Murder Memoir Murder is a memoir and a crime novel involving a hunt for a missing IRA informer, set in the

Ne hope you enjoy this bo
renew it by the due date.

D0512897

You can renew it at www.n
by using our free library app

Otherwise you can phone 0344 800 8020 -
please have your library card and PIN ready.

You can sign up for email reminders too.

NORFOLK COUNTY COUNCIL
LIBRARY AND INFORMATION SERVICE

For more information visit. www.anthonyjquinnwriter.com

Murder
Memoir
Murder

Anthony J. Quinn

Dalzell Press

First published in 2022 by Dalzell Press

Dalzell Press
54 Abbey Street
Bangor, N. Ireland BT20 4JB

© Anthony J. Quinn 2022

ISBN 978-1-8380871-4-2

Cover Design: Karen Vaughn

Supported by the National Lottery though the Arts
Council of Northern Ireland

LOTTERY FUNDED

For my mother and father.

2019

Lough Derg was purgatory, an otherworldly place that revealed itself to me less as rocks and water than as light, an eerie light brimming with reflections and shadows.

Early in the afternoon, I waited with the other pilgrims for the boat to Station Island, a swarm of midges enveloping us with an aggressive frenzy, each one of us attracting our own column of insects in the way magnets attract iron filings. I was tired and hungry and just looking at the lough through the grey fuzz of flies reminded me that I was heading towards a place of suffering.

When the boat arrived, we walked towards it with the uncertain gait of sleepwalkers. From the cabin, the boatman appeared, blocking the gangway. At first, it seemed he wasn't going to let us board, and then I realised he had stepped out to finish a cigarette. He took a deep drag, and with a smoky sigh, tossed the butt into the dark waters. "The midges on the island are worse," he warned. "These ones have only one set of teeth."

I don't like travelling, much less travelling on my own to gloomy places like Lough Derg, but there was someone on the island I had to meet. A person who needed my help. I was also hoping to find some inspiration that would rejuvenate my writing career, which a year previously had ground to a complete halt. I liked travelling as an idea, especially the notion that I might be a pilgrim crossing physical and imaginary borders to an island specially equipped to welcome my soul. Travelling as a parable, a journey across the divisions between good and evil, the past and the present. But the first cracks had already appeared in my vision of this perfect island.

The boatman revved the engine and then we set out into deep water. I stared at the other passengers swaying blindly to the motion of the boat. I feared there would be no cure for me on the island, just the bewildered faces of other lost souls and two days of trials, endless prayer, and hunger. I hadn't come to pray, and I wondered would the priests spot that I was a fraud, an impostor. But wasn't writing an act of faith, too? A year previously, I had given up my job as a reporter, killing off a career in journalism and a reliable wage to concentrate on writing fiction. Like the pilgrims, I was searching for meaning. My meaning came from stories, and I was hungry for them, the kind of secret stories that exist as whispers, so quiet they resemble the faintest of breaths, and are heard only in hushed places like lonely islands and church confessionals. Stories rather than prayers were my obsession. I had concluded that if I wasn't writing or searching for a story, I was doing nothing.

A few seagulls escorted the boat as we spun out into the lough, which stretched before us like a vast sheet of silver. A black wall of deformed pine trees rose along the Donegal shore, and then a rugged chain of hills and mountains took over, covered in more trees and heather, the shades of blue and purple merging and growing deeper towards the horizon. We were the only intruders in a landscape completely devoid of people, houses, cars, or farm animals. In sharp contrast, the island we were heading towards was packed with church buildings, like the thin remnants of an ecclesiastical city that had survived a great flood. Within its precincts, I could make out a throng of shuffling stick-like figures.

Bitter thoughts of what lay ahead constricted my heart, the fatigue and hunger I would be exposing myself to, the long night of barefoot walking through a labyrinth of prayer and worries about what was I going to say to the person I had arranged to meet. How would we pass the long hours of silence and darkness together?

The sound of the waves washing against the boat changed, the temperature dropped, and a feeling of expectation grew on the boat. It began raining. Somehow, the raindrops seemed larger and more transparent than the rain in Belfast. The downpour thickened, beating so heavily it churned the flat surface of the lough into a sweep of disturbed gravel. When it stopped, I stood up and crossed to the bow of the boat. I was aware of the other passengers watching me with curiosity as I leaned over the railings and stared at the breaking wave. I indulged myself with the notion that I was flying, the reflections of the clouds ridging on the water below strengthening the illusion. I leaned out further and followed the reflection of the hidden sun, its weak glow creeping like an oily sea creature alongside the boat. The sound of waterfowl rippled out from an inlet, and I felt a stab of loneliness.

Soon, our destination swung into view. First the monolithic octagonal basilica, followed by the oppressive grey dormitory that looked as though it could serve as a medium size prison, and the buildings' eerily extravagant reflections on the smooth lough. The light in the sky strengthened, giving a shine to our arrival as the boat ghosted into the island's narrow bay. When I stared at the monastic waters, I could see another island trapped beneath glass, a darker tier in the labyrinth. The goose pimples tightened on my arms and shoulders.

A young man, who might have been a student priest, greeted us and led the way to the dormitories. He pointed in two directions, men in the left wing, and women in the right wing. He performed his duties with the minimum of communication and fuss, giving me a ticket with a number on it. The tickets were now our official form of identity. Later they would be used to allocate our daily meal of black tea and toast.

I found my bed in a cubicle with three other bunk beds. I took off my shoes and socks and placed them underneath the bed. From now until the third morning, I would be barefoot. The dormitory was chilly and austere with its bare walls and rows of bunk beds housed in cubicles, but somehow, I found the dispiriting atmosphere soothing. The high lead-paned windows, the narrow corridors and the stairwells swamped in darkness gave me a comforting sense of confinement. I was now an inmate of an institution for people hankering to be good and saintly, hidden away on a lough of gloomy water and secret islands. Even the idea of giving up my shoes and socks for the next two days felt secretly pleasing.

Rather than join the other newcomers on their first walkabout along the island's prayer paths, I set off in search of the person I had come to meet. Another boat arrived, and the island filled with more pilgrims. The sociable murmur of their prayers passed from group to group so intensely that at times it sounded as though a delicious piece of gossip were doing the rounds. I paced amid the pilgrims, at cross-purposes to their shuffling, moving between them as though trying to find a path through a maze. Some of them had sat down and were dozing. I bumped into a traveller woman sitting alone, talking to herself in between bouts of croaking laughter. She kept exclaiming, "The midges are eating me alive," and, "Oh, my poor feet are burning."

I looked down and was met by a sea of tired-looking feet. Never before had I seen so many swollen ankles and cracked soles with patches of thickened skin and bunions angling this way and that in the mud, reddened toes feeling for leverage on the sharp stones. Undaunted, determined to find my contact, I threaded my way through the labyrinth of squirming feet.

On the eastern tip of the island, I came across an elderly woman sitting on a bench overlooking the lough. She remained motionless as I studied her. I thought she might be asleep or dead, or one of those figures that belong to another dimension. When I drew closer, she looked up. The light and happiness that filled her face when she saw me seemed otherworldly. For the first time on my journey, I smiled. The island was full of old people, moving around in companionable groups, but she was completely alone. What was it about this person who by simply gazing at me with such a glow in her eyes made all my troubles vanish?

She was my mother. Hers was the face I always sought as a child when I had been startled out of sleep by the recurring nightmare of the IRA murdering my father, hers was the hand I sought to hold me, and which now as the father of three children, I feared would cling to me and pull me back into the shadows of the past.

"You made it through the night?" I asked.

"Yes."

I was playing the role of dutiful son, come to check that she had survived the first night of constant praying and walking on an empty stomach. I sat down at an awkward angle beside her. I had another reason for visiting the island, and I felt there was something slightly grubby about my posing as a pilgrim before her, even though I only had a vague idea of the story I was searching for and had no intention of entrapping or betraying anyone. Certainly not the island itself and its holy traditions.

"Well done, you've twenty-four hours behind you," I said. "Out of how many, forty-eight?"

"It's easier to count the prayers than the hours."

My guilt went straight to the set of rosary beads clasped in her hands. I had barely touched mine. "Sorry, were you praying?"

"No, I've finished my last station."

She grabbed my wrist. She wanted me to go to the canteen and have some black tea and toast with her. She had been waiting for me before she had hers, and so, like an obliging son, I followed and joined the queue of pilgrims trudging through the canteen doors.

Inside, I expected a noisy clamouring for food, but instead everyone was silent and respectful of each other, waiting politely and passing the plates of toast to their neighbours. Soon the canteen filled with swarming shadows, munching resolutely and whispering, everyone reluctant to disturb the hush. We sat down on a long wooden bench. My mother insisted on pouring the tea and watched with a smile as I sipped it. She reached over and placed a plate of dry toast in front of me. Then she handed me a Pilgrim Exercise leaflet, which contained a map for visitors to acquaint themselves with the paths and the topography of the island, and a list of the different rituals we had to complete over the two days.

On the eastern side of the island lay St Patrick's Basilica, and in front of it an iron cross dedicated to St Patrick. Further west sat the penitential beds, the remnants of beehive cells used by ancient monks, which formed the focus of the nine stations or praying rituals. She told me how to walk and pray three times around the outside of each cell, and three times around the inside. At each station, there were nine points where you had to kneel, and then, at St Patrick's Cross, you had to kneel twice. Three of the stations we had to perform before nightfall, four during the night in the basilica, and the final two on the second day. She warned me not to sit or lie on my dormitory bed until ten pm the following evening in case I accidentally fell asleep. Even here, on an island where everyone was equal as pilgrims, I was not on a level field with her.

We watched the steam rise from our cups and fill the room with a grey light. I listened to her account of the night before, how she had struggled valiantly with her arthritis along the stony prayer paths. I looked briefly into her shining eyes, and then looked away. A man had rudely woken her when she accidentally fell asleep, shaking her sore shoulder with a rough hand. I felt a protective flash of anger. In contrast to her injured words, her expression was happy, and her eyes full of light. Was it the effect of fasting and avoiding sleep? I began to hope the island might make it easier for her to open up about the past and answer the questions on my mind.

We sat there and I grew alert to the things conveyed soundlessly, the deeper conversations between us not linked in any way to the words we expressed. With my mother, it always felt as though we were skirting something important and interesting, unlike my chats with my father, which were full of common sense, grounded in reality and often bordering on the meaningless, not only his comments, but mine, too. My father and I talked like genial strangers, seeking some form of reassurance that we knew each other, or shared a common ground, and, afterwards, little of what we said was remembered or mulled over. By contrast, my mother's conversations came from a different place and exerted a strange pull that was impossible to fight against. Often, the feeling I had afterwards, deep in the pit of my stomach, was one of uneasiness.

The pilgrims began swarming out of the canteen, everyone at pains not to interrupt or bump into each other. Many of them were on their second day like my mother. Their bodies were tired and sore. Yet they moved with dignity, talking under their breaths and respecting the hunger of others. The room emptied, and we were on our own. We stared at our bare feet as though they didn't belong to us. In the silence, I tried to work out the chemistry between this devout woman, an only child, who had been raised by her father on a lonely farm on the Irish Border, and me, her eldest son. I sifted through the multitude of blessings and coercions that characterised our relationship. Why, in conversation, did I raise particular subjects and not others? Why I asked her virtually no questions about the past and always rushed to reassure her that it had been an idyllic childhood with my four siblings growing up on a small farm in South Tyrone during the Troubles. Why did certain sorrows and sufferings always hide behind the stories we told of the past, stories that were plucked out of nowhere and aimed at making us smile or laugh or to soothe our worries about the future. What if we could, for just one afternoon, confront the past as equals, rather than as mother and son?

It was typical that she had drawn me to this island full of prayer and hardship, obliging me to take part in a pilgrimage I was not sure I wanted to do, but had been talking vaguely about for months. Or was it my discontent that had dragged me here? I wanted to tell her the story of my hopeless novel and its failed hero, the never-ending emptiness of the white page, how I was in danger of caring about nothing else, that beyond breaking my writer's block I had no other goal, no other reason to keep going on. I had given up paid employment to dedicate my time to writing a detective novel set during the Troubles. Every crime novel poses its own technical problems, which have to be resolved by the plot and the deductions of the detective figure, but my detective didn't seem to have much talent for investigating, or was it the writer who lacked the talent?

My mother's body relaxed, and her eyelids drooped. She was falling asleep. I touched her shoulder gently, and she stiffened. She blinked at me with a look of annoyance. I had robbed her of the joy of sleep. Then she smiled.

"Tell me a story about my grandfather," I asked.

She hesitated. She had many stories about her father, but I had in mind one in particular. A story that might cure my writer's block. My grandfather as an eleven-year-old boy in the last light of a June evening, trudging home from a bog at Cappagh with a donkey and a cart heavily loaded with turf. My grandfather as an exhausted farmer's son summoning his remaining strength to turn the final corner home, and then stopping, transfixed by the sight of men with guns loitering at the side of the road. The story of how and why my grandfather never made it home that evening.

It was the time of the Irish Civil War, and my

grandfather's neighbours were fighting in a war, a shadowy underground conflict that pitted brothers against brothers, fathers against sons. However, the political context, the frame of reference was lost to my grandfather's family. The farm they lived on in Diseart had fallen heavily into debt, the financial bind forcing his father, Thomas Daly, to travel to Scotland in search of work, leaving my grandfather as the eldest son to carry out all the farm jobs. Weeks and months had gone by with letters containing money arriving in the post, but then the letters stopped. The family assumed that Thomas must have died in some sort of accident or from an illness, but there never was a farewell note, or a body or any kind of funeral, just a vague story from a cattle dealer that he had died in a lodging house somewhere in Perth.

When my grandfather rounded the final bend in the road that day, heroically hauling home a winter's load of turf, the men with guns were waiting to interrogate him. They were members of the Royal Irish Constabulary, dressed in dark green uniforms, and they were hunting for a murderer. In the gentle summer twilight, their figures must have seemed sinister, spectral even, to my grandfather's exhausted eyes, and what followed must have felt like a bad dream, as he let go of the donkey's reins and their figures approached. They fired questions at him, and he answered them. They spotted blood on his fingernails and asked more questions. Then they searched his coat and found a heavily bloodstained handkerchief. He told them that he suffered from nosebleeds, but they arrested him anyway on suspicion of murder, or being an accessory to murder, holding him in the police station in Ballygawley for two days.

My mother had told me the story only once, in a whisper, and almost in spite of herself, around the time the

IRA held us at gunpoint and hijacked our car. But even as a boy, part of me had thought that the story didn't quite tally, and that my mother or her father must have been hiding something. There were gaps in the story, shadows that had sown a tiny seed of doubt in my mind. My grandfather, who wouldn't harm a fly, whose one addiction, his one luxury, was his Catholic faith, how could he have ever been suspected of killing a human being? What had prompted her to tell me such a story in the first place? Was it to draw attention away from something else, a trauma in the present? Had the mistaken arrest foreshadowed another dark event in the parish?

Sitting with my mother on that uncomfortable bench, I didn't know how to bring the conversation round to the story, so I just started talking about it, hoping that I could remember the sequence of events correctly. The day before my grandfather's arrest, the body of a neighbour called Tom Donaghy, an IRA man, had been found beaten to death and covered in blood. The finger of blame had fallen on local members of the Hibernian Society, fellow Catholics, who espoused less violent ideals than the IRA, and to which my grandfather belonged as a junior member. In spite of the police investigation, no one was ever convicted of Donaghy's murder, and a wall of silence formed around the killing.

"How could they have suspected a boy of murder?" I asked her. In my mind, it all sounded like a terrible mistake, or a bad joke. A boy staggering home with a load of turf, trying to run a gorse-infested farm for his mother, three siblings and his lost father. A boy not afraid of hard work, full of innocence and good intentions. What evidence did they have other than the blood on his fingernails and the handkerchief to support such a wild suspicion? And why were they waiting for him at the corner of the road in the first place?

"Who told you that story?" asked my mother, the warmth in her eyes evaporating.

"You."

"When?" She crooked her mouth into a frown.

"One night when I was around eleven."

She didn't respond. Had she forgotten? In the silence, I thought of a question to ask, something to lighten the mood, but she spoke first.

"Aren't there better stories to talk about?"

But I had heard all the good stories about my grandfather. They had been repeated countless times around the fire and at family gatherings. I didn't want to hear the stories my family knew off by heart. I wanted to hear the stories locked away in the past, the stories that we didn't know we knew and could only come to know by asking questions of shadowy ghosts and listening to silences. What were the police doing investigating with such apparent thoroughness the murder of an IRA man? Weren't they sworn enemies? Was my grandfather's arrest a cruel little circus orchestrated to prove the police were treating the murder seriously? There might even have been a more sinister motivation, to deflect attention away from the true suspects, and what they put my grandfather through was a contortion of justice, the only form of investigation the dead man's family could expect from a hostile police force.

"Did he ever explain why the police were waiting for him? I can't understand what made them decide to interrogate an eleven-year-old boy."

"He never talked about it."

"What about his mother, his neighbours, the members of the Hibernian society, how did they react?"

"He never said anything."

My grandfather loved telling stories and he must have known in his heart that the only way to keep the truth of that day intact was by not talking about it. Stories are told and retold; they grow and shed their skin according to the mood of the teller and the audience. They develop different versions and become many stories. My grandfather had guarded the truth about his arrest all his life.

I hesitated, hoping she had more to tell me. She seemed lost as if sifting through remote thoughts. I waited to see if she would return with one.

"It was strange…"

"What was strange?"

"You know your grandfather never liked talking about the past. He preferred company, playing cards and saying his prayers. He prayed for hours every night by the fire."

"I know. I dreaded walking in on him when he was saying the rosary. Do you remember how he always dedicated the third decade to the conversion of China?"

"I still have his prayer book." Her eyes glowed, but I could see a shadow of sadness there. Was it for her father's lost childhood or her own? "He said the same prayers every single night of his life. The pages are indented and black with the mark of his thumbs. You have to come over and look at it. See for yourself."

She had shown me the prayer book before. It was one of her most treasured possessions. And what she said was true. You could touch the book and feel the pressure marks of her father's thumbs where he gripped the same pages every night. She proceeded to tell me a poignant story about her childhood, which I hesitate to write because it's unlikely to have any bearing on this story.

My mother was an only child. When she was six, her mother suffered a mental breakdown after being knocked down by a bus, and she spent the rest of her life locked up in an asylum. My mother must have been very lonely as a child, but she never said so. She was at peace with that little six-year-old girl who must have missed her mother terribly. My mother had five children, and I imagine that the memory of her early loneliness must have sometimes felt like a refuge. Her father was a patient and peaceable man, prone to melancholy in the winter, and she had no one to boss her around or over-protect her. She and he had a silent form of communication. She often said that he could look right through her as though she were water and figure out exactly what feelings or thoughts she was trying to hide. She complained she could keep nothing from him.

"But what was strange?" I tried to bring her back to her original thought.

She gave me a blank look before the memory returned. "Oh, yes, all his life, he never talked about the arrest. But after the IRA hijacked our car, he changed."

"How?"

"It seemed so out of character. He got very upset and mentioned the day he had the nosebleed. He was worried about you."

"Me? Why?"

"It was after the IRA handed you the bullet for your dad. You were eleven at the time. The same age he was when he was arrested. He thought you wanted to run away."

My grandfather must have confused my childhood for his. In his old age, watching me and my siblings play in the same fields he toiled over as a boy, the two childhoods must have felt like parallel worlds, his eleven-year-old self eternally trudging home in a maze of back roads.

I put my mind to work and thought of the IRA men who hijacked our family car and held us at gunpoint that spring morning in 1982. My poor mother had been convinced they were loyalist paramilitaries come to shoot my father. Instead, they took the car and used it as the getaway vehicle to shoot a police officer dead. To ensure my parents did not tip off the security forces, one of the IRA men handed me a gold-coloured bullet before they left. He warned me he would use it to shoot my father, if my parents contacted the police before the appointed time. It was a small moment in the tumult of a mad morning, but one I remember vividly. At first, I thought the IRA man had wanted to shake my hand. A conscientious child, I accepted the bullet, and held it carefully until the IRA departed. I knew it carried an important message. I gave it to my mother, who wrapped it up tightly in an old sweetie wrapper and then hid it.

Part of me had always wanted to meet that IRA man again and ask him about the decisions he made that morning. Why not give the bullet to my father or mother, instead? Why single me out among my siblings? Did he remember how our paths crossed or had he forgotten the frightened boy and the bullet he'd pressed into his hands? Perhaps he'd handed out bullets to lots of people and never considered the stories that would form around them and the things the recipients would think through the years, remembering the cold feel of the bullet in their hands. I had changed since then, got an education, built a house and started a family but what had happened to him? Had he changed? The story I heard from my parents was that one day he left everything and disappeared. I suspected he was dead now, but what if he were still alive? I could track him down and talk to him, ask him some questions and listen to his answers. And even if I didn't find him, my search would be a story in itself.

I knew so little about the IRA man. I'd only seen his

eyes, mouth and some reddish facial hair sticking out from under his balaclava. But there were places I could go to find out more, and people I could ask, neighbours and contacts from the world of journalism. An idea for a book formed in my mind. I saw the masked face of the IRA man rising before me, like a mysterious genie, summoned to help break my writer's block. The genie who had given me the gift of a bullet, and who would now give me a story. For the first time ever, the memory of his oddly gleaming eyes did not give me a sense of dread. Instead, I felt inspired and the more I thought about his eyes, the more they seemed to glow with the same strange excitement I was feeling.

I remembered some vague talk about the IRA man being a relative of Donaghy. Another question formed in my mind, one that had always nagged me. Were the hijacking and the arrest linked? One a punishment or a reprisal for the other? As a child, I had not been aware of how many plots were operating at the heart of our parish, how many secrets flowed like hidden currents between families. I felt my head expand in a further wave of excitement. Then I checked myself. It felt wrong to think about these two unsolved murders as the basis of a book. But then, what was right in the secret history of the Troubles? And if I didn't write about the two killings, wouldn't their secrets disappear into the mists of time?

"Do you think the hijacking and granddad's arrest were linked?" I asked.

She looked at me sharply. Had she realised I was already enrolling her in the plot of a book? She got up and walked away.

"I'm tired," she said.

I was tired, too. I shouldn't have started probing the past. It was a mistake. I got to my feet and followed her.

"What made you think that?" she asked. She stepped over a large uneven stone and reached out. Instinctively, I offered her my arm. She held on and then released me. Her hand felt cold, and I could sense her fatigue. It was the tiredness of a woman who had been driven by the fear of loneliness all her life.

"I don't know," I said. "As a child, I must have joined the two things together. The IRA men coming into our house with guns and the policemen arresting granddad."

She lowered her head in her shoulders and looked up at the heavy sky where the evening sun was trying to break through. June sun in Ireland, so cold and distant on cloudy days that it barely warmed the skin. I felt there was something more she wanted to say. Something she was keeping from me. We wandered along the paths. For a while, we stared at the black wall of pine trees on the opposite shore. I had never seen her look so tired before. She looked like who she was, a seventy-year-old woman driven by a vision of a happy family life unstained by the Troubles, a woman who had raised five children and still felt responsible for their welfare. I wanted to give her something, a sense of peace and closure about the past, but instead I kept pushing.

"Maybe the people who murdered Donaghy never intended to kill him. It might have been a drunken fight that got out of hand?"

Caution took hold of her. There was sadness in her eyes, but also wariness.

"No, they planned it," she said.

Our conversation went off in another direction. She told me about a long-lost relative whom she'd managed to track down to the U.S., and how they were planning a reunion. She was forever tracking down lost cousins, and always had a new story about the family tree to recount, usually involving a wayward uncle, an illegitimate child or an alcoholic father. Sometimes, I wasn't sure if she had found the right people, whether they were actual relatives or complete strangers turning up at her door. But it didn't seem to matter to her or to them. For years, she had been researching our family history, creating stories and connections out of practically nothing, mere shadows and rumours.

"That's good," I said, trying to sound interested. I didn't want to hear stories about distant relations. They meant nothing to me and the story I wanted to write. My grandfather had worked all that day, stacking turf on his cart. His family were depending on him, and the winters were long, dark and cold. A ten-mile journey along a mountain road full of mud and holes lay ahead of him. Many times, he must have thought he would never make it, when the cart swayed over potholes, or the donkey refused to move. He had no resources other than the will of an eleven-year-old boy, determined to take the place of his father, a determination full of bravery and instinctive duty. Wasn't the meaning of his handkerchief clear? It was stained with the blood of an eleven-year-old boy, stained with his determination and purity, nothing else.

I fell deep into thought, and then my mother's placid voice reached me.

"What are you thinking about?

Her question surprised me. "I don't know. I'm trying to work out my next book."

"What sort of book?" She tilted her head so she could look into my eyes.

I hesitated. She knew I was always working on a new book, that when I finished one, I felt oppressed by a dissatisfaction so great that all I could do to ease it was to start writing another one. What sort of book was I writing?

A book that would save my writing career or at least prolong it for another year or two. A book whose plot and characters I was trying to wring out of the past.

"Another crime novel?" she asked.

"No, not this time." Wasn't everyone writing crime novels these days? Good writers, mediocre writers, bad writers, even celebrities and politicians.

"What about writing a book about a saint?" she asked.

"Oliver Plunkett would be perfect. You could write about his beheading and how he was hung, drawn and quartered."

"Yes, maybe it's time I wrote about somebody good."

Perhaps my grandfather's bloody handkerchief was the most innocent thing in the world that day. Perhaps the only secrets or surprises in the story were decent, noble ones. I felt a tension rising in my chest. I had to solve the clue of the handkerchief, carry out some form of investigation into the past, but I didn't know what it was or how to proceed, only that I had to head in a certain direction and keep going until I reached a page with the words 'The End' printed at the bottom.

"Whatever you do, just keep writing, don't ever stop," said my mother. Her smile had grown stern, mouth down turned, her hand clutching the rosary beads. She stared at me with a familiar expression of reproof, which was her way of communicating encouragement.

I shuddered at the cruelty of what had awaited my grandfather on the last turn of the road, the blind suspicion of the policemen, who spotted his bloodstained fingernails and found the handkerchief, their resistance to reason and common-sense, arresting him on the spot and transporting him to the police station without informing his mother. I thought of the stubbornness of blood blindly pouring from a wound and the killers eluding justice. I thought of the stains that persist, an unsolved murder and a god-fearing parish stumbling in its wake, the litany of rumours and ignorant suspicions that I was already turning into metaphors for a story.

"So, no more crime fiction?" said my mother.

"Yes. No more detective novels. Something to do with real life this time. About the Troubles."

"A true story?"

"Not quite." The only kind of truth I was interested in was one that would save me from writer's block. "Sometimes the telling of the story is more important than the truth."

"Why write a story like that?"

"What do you mean?"

"Why write a story but not tell the truth?"

Damn the truth. It didn't enter into it. What did I want? Literary approval? Commercial success? I knew that I didn't want to write another crime novel, but was I capable of doing anything else? I did not know. I only thought of breaking my writer's block. For the last year, my thoughts and feelings had been enveloped in a vague, grey fog. I kept putting words together and hoping for the best, but nothing stuck. Each day's empty page was added to the previous day's, and no matter how hard I tried, I felt and thought nothing. For the first time in years, I had nothing. I was no longer writing. I was avoiding life.

"Because I only want the story," I said.

"But not the reality?"

What kind of book would that make? The reality of the Troubles. Pages and pages of grim, unreadable chaos.

My mother sighed. "Your grandfather said we would all be dead before the Troubles ended, because the Troubles were never going to end."

A thought formed in my head. Silences and evasions

were more enthralling than the truth. The facts, if I ever could retrieve them, were irrelevant. It was the search for the facts that excited me, and the lies that were just as important as the truths. A collection of lies might be the best expression of the Troubles, the most definitive story of the past. Plutarch had quoted something similar about the power of Greek tragedies: 'He who deceives is more honest than he who does not deceive, and he who is deceived is wiser than he who is not deceived.' But did I really believe that? And what good would it do anyway to write about lies and silences? Would they really help anyone to know anything more about themselves or the Troubles? What about my own lies and evasions? What had I neglected or ignored in my own life that needed attention? The questions lodged themselves in my mind and made me feel uneasy.

"What's wrong?" she asked.

"Nothing."

"You look as though something's upset you."

"Nothing's upset me."

Beyond us, in the gloom of the basilica, the chant of the evening stations began, hushed but insistent. The pilgrims I had arrived with were beginning their long night of praying, while others were retiring to their beds. It was time for my mother to get some sleep, too.

"I have to go now," she said. "You should start your first station as soon as you can. Before the tiredness sets in."

I nodded.

"Will you say a few prayers for everyone in the family?" she asked.

"I'll say a rosary for us all."

She looked serene as I watched her leave, walking lightly to her bed, like a woman already dreaming.

I was alone now and had time and silence to think. I walked the prayer paths as the evening light dwindled. I picked up holy books in the entrance hall of the little church next to the dormitory but did not read them. I sat on a bench and stared at the darkening lough. I was cut off from my children, my wife and the rest of the world. I had no idea of what was happening on social media. The only reality I cared about was that conjured up by the first paragraph of my new book, the story that had been waiting to enthral me, hiding at the heart of my family. I had much less proof or evidence than a journalist would need to start writing the story. In fact, I had no proof at all, just my faith, which was a different form of faith to that of the pilgrims. However, like them, I had no desire to dedicate my thoughts to something that could be easily proved or was blindingly obvious to even the most ignorant fool.

Night drew in. I grew tired of sitting on my own and the urge to join in the pilgrim's experience strengthened. I mumbled a few offerings, and the loneliness of not belonging eased as my bare feet felt their way along the stones. I curled my toes around the uneven edges and started moving in accordance with the set prayers, surreptitiously studying the movements of the pilgrims in front of me, shuffling and kneeling on the paths. I tried to look as if I knew what I was doing, planting my bare feet on the wet grass and the sharp stones, joining the circles of pilgrims as they trudged the furrows worn out by their ancestors.

I followed the stations, letting so much time elapse at each cell before moving on so that my thoughts might not burden the little groups of people assembled there. I placed myself in a kind of quarantine, afraid of showing my face to the same pilgrims for too long, lest they enquire about where I was from or why I was doing the pilgrimage.

At one point, I looked up and saw a small priest standing next to St Patrick's Cross with his dark eyes on me. Who or what was he? Some sort of frowning troll guarding the site? I could sense his eyes inspect me. Had he noticed the uncertainty in my praying, the unwillingness converted into clumsiness as I clambered over the stone paths?

I crept into the basilica and took a seat at the back. I stared for a long time at the candles winking in the gloom of the altar and the dark motion of the pilgrims shuffling through their stations. The excitement had diminished, but I could still feel a small glow of contentment. The restlessness of the faithful and the churning wash of the waves outside the basilica somehow helped me focus my thoughts. Two unsolved murders, two families left without justice, and a web of connections hidden at the heart of a parish. Wasn't that the sort of story that deserved to be told, a mystery that had never been properly explained?

On one level, I felt an odd sense of peace, even satisfaction, thinking of the invisible seams that connected the two tragedies. I saw myself renewed as a writer, no longer frustrated and silent, following clues into the past. But what sort of son did that make me? Prowling after my mother along these paths, sniffing out the details of a family secret, my heart full of grinding literary ambition. And what about the initial wave of inspiration? How long would that last? I felt motivated to start writing immediately, but how would I feel after ten thousand words? I thought of the rumours and half-remembered stories I would have to sift through, the obstacles that I would have to negotiate. What if I kept digging and digging, doggedly following the trail, but only met a wall of silence? Wouldn't that leave me feeling more frustrated than before? Was it worth the risk of embarrassing or hurting her and my neighbours?

I thought of all the troubles that would come home to roost if the book were ever published. The fury of affronted parishioners who would have every right to feel upset if I mentioned their names or those of their dead relatives. In order to write about Donaghy's murder, I would have to set the scene, frame it in a certain way, include certain details and ignore others. In other words, I would have to set myself up as the judge of all that had happened that day and the cover-ups that followed.

I thought of my mother's face reading the passages about her and her father. The anger and shock etched on her features. I glanced up at the stained-glass windows and stared at the dull gleam of Jesus' body stretched out on the cross. I saw myself on stage, in the spotlight, an author arrogantly exposing his family and his neighbours' secrets, while his mother wept in the wings.

Or would she? Might she be glad I had written such a book? A search for the truth about a murder, a murder that would explain everything that happened afterwards in the parish and the hidden connections between its families. A murder that was the prelude to another killing, the pendulum of history swinging from one date to the other. I would follow the pendulum to the top of the arc and then back the other way. And afterwards, when I had written the book, I would let my mother read it and cut out anything that annoyed her. I did not want to annoy anyone, not even myself, but what sort of writer did that make me?

One part of me thought it would be better if the story ended here, and another was tempted by the thought that this was just the beginning. The questions hung in the air along with the pungent smell of incense. I leaned forwards and rubbed my face with my hands. I had a difficult decision ahead of me. But I was going to make it one way or the other, and after I had made it, would I still have writer's block? I did not know. All I knew was that I could no longer live with empty pages.

I slipped out of the pew, hurried away from the pilgrims and made my way down to the dark shore. I raised my eyes to the lough's restless waters and the night sky, my thoughts hovering with the waves and the heaving shapes they moulded out of the darkness. Why was I so in thrall to shadows and silences?

The bell began to sound, calling everyone to Mass in the basilica and bringing me back to my senses. The pathways emptied of pilgrims, but I was reluctant to join them. I found a way of keeping out of sight, clinging to the water's edge and squeezing myself into one of the many dark crannies with secret views of the lough. I wanted to be alone with my thoughts rather than herded in with the others.

Eventually, an eager young priest found me and told me that Mass had started and that I must hurry to the church. I told him I did not need to go to Mass and would not be convinced otherwise. He went off and promptly returned with the elderly prior, a short man with bullish eyes, who regarded me suspiciously.

"Are you a pilgrim?" he asked.

After some hesitation, I answered. "Yes, I am."

"The pilgrims," he said, "are in the church." With a confidence and authority that reflected his control of the island and all its visitors, he extended his hand in the direction of the basilica.

1982

The morning of the IRA hijacking began with the piping of bird song. Alice Quinn rose early, lit the range, cleaned the kitchen, ironed the children's clothes, laid the breakfast table with a mixed assortment of bowls, and poured fresh milk from one of her father's cows into a glass jug. By the time the children pushed themselves out of bed and entered the kitchen, bleary-eyed and uncertain in their pyjamas, the place glittered and basked in the warm light of dawn.

The first in were the oldest pair, followed by the middle daughter, and then the youngest two. She liked seeing her children's downturned faces on these bright spring mornings, their hair ruffled into airy balls by sleep, their expressions shy, grumpy, true, their voices that little bit throatier than usual. She marched them to the range where she filled their bowls with porridge.

When breakfast was over, she washed the dishes at the window. From the corner of her eye, she saw a pair of dark birds streaking from the hedge, outlined in the low sunlight. Carefully, she scrubbed the pots, working the fibres of the cleaning pad along the bottom rim, rinsing as she scrubbed, removing the dregs and specks of congealed porridge. It was such a fine morning. The air was completely still, the trees stood completely still, and the back garden, lit by the suspended rays of the sun, resembled a painting. Yet something had disturbed the two birds. She placed the pot on the drying rack and turned to her children, who were carrying their bowls with outstretched arms and dumping them in the sink. She started on the bowls, but her thoughts were elsewhere. Her eyes had retained an image of the birds leaping from the hedge. Song thrushes, of course. That was what they were. She unplugged the sink, and the warm water was sucked through her fingers into the drain. But what had unsettled the birds?

In the darkest corner of the garden, where the boxwood and holly lost themselves to the wildness of a blackthorn hedge, she glimpsed something moving, a crawling lump of shadows. She paused, slowly drying her hands. Her skin tingled with coldness. The shadows grew into a group of human figures, heads lowered, weaving through the thorns and briars. She stood completely still, feeling the jostle of her children around her, the small collisions of their bodies, waves and ripples that tugged at her attention. The figures in the hedge were moving quickly now, flickering along the back of the garden. She searched for faces but saw only masks and the glint of guns.

She took in the swift shadows of men running and dropped the dishes. She did not know what the gunmen were planning, but she knew they were about to cross the threshold of her home. She saw their weapons and understood their determination, their will to use violence and instil fear. She grabbed as many of her children as she could and fled from the window, calling the others after her. With a sickening sense of horror, she bundled them into the tiny hot-press closet at the bottom of the corridor, tearing down the piles of sheets and blankets upon them. Then she squeezed herself in, pulled the door shut and leaned her body against it. She went through all the possibilities in her head. Her worst fear was that the gunmen were intent on shooting her husband dead.

For years, Catholic men had been dying violently in

their bedrooms and front halls, across the green parishes of Tyrone. The murders, carried out by the Ulster Volunteer Force, were sectarian, and justified as reprisals for IRA attacks on police officers and soldiers, part of a mindless cycle of tit-for-tat killings. Death stalked isolated farmhouses and dark country lanes, preying upon the living and demanding revenge. This was why she chose to stay hidden with her children while her husband, who had been working late the night before, slept on in their bedroom. She felt them around her in the darkness and wanted to save and protect them at all costs. She emptied her thoughts into prayers to the Virgin Mary.

She heard the front door open and heavy footsteps enter the hall. Nothing more happened. A hand tugged her blouse. She turned and felt her youngest son bury his head in her stomach. She held him in a moment of utter stillness. She thought wait, just a few minutes more. She closed her eyes, took a deep breath, and inhaled the fresh scents of the laundered sheets that rustled as her children made tiny movements in the overheated closet. She had left her husband's fate in the hands of the gunmen. She felt as though she were ransoming his life by not warning him of the danger in time. She was allowing the gunmen to take him so that she might save her children. She waited for the deathly rattle of gunfire, but there was only silence.

2019

I put down my pen, closed my notebook and slipped outside to sniff the twilight air, leaving the side door open, a boot wedged next to the hinge, in the hope that the shadows of the night would somehow creep into the house and lend my writing the proper atmosphere. Absent-mindedly, I wandered through the trees that swept down to the road at the front of the house. Tiny bats swooped and darted overhead, too deeply immersed in their pursuit of insects to notice my restless walk. The couples who strolled past the house every evening, pausing to look neither left nor right, had all returned to their homes. Beyond the empty road, the narrow glen lay full of shadows.

There was something deliberate in the sounds of the swaying branches and rustling leaves, but their whispering stirred nothing in me. I was too deep inside my thoughts. This emptiness I felt should have worried me. It was too soon and too overwhelming. But I told myself it was part of the writing process and I'd had many nights like these before. There would be long nights of empty pages and blank thoughts ahead. This wouldn't be the first. I could be sure of that.

Ten years ago, I moved back to this secluded hollow in the foothills of the Sperrin mountains with my wife, Frances, and our three children. On the hill to the right, I could see, through the trees, the lights of the rambling farmhouse belonging to my parents, Alice and Dermot, now in their mid-70s, and the darkening lane where we often greeted each other and chatted. There were other lights deeper amid the trees. Lights that I could only see in winter when the leaves of the beech, hazel and ash trees fell, the lights of the homes where three of my sisters also lived with their young families.

The only sounds of the world were the distant roar of lorries carried several miles by the south-westerly winds. I looked at the pine trees, dark strokes against the sky, lying thick to the south, filling the glen where I could walk for ages without meeting another soul. In moving back here, to the place where I'd grown up, I'd wanted to surrender to the emptiness of this wild glen at twilight, leaving everything, all my worries and fears, in the shadows of its trees swaying in the evening breezes. It was strange the forces that I felt emanating from the twilight landscape, but they were good. For a decade, as I helped raise our children and worked as a reporter for the local newspaper, I wrote every evening, nine novels in total, wrapping myself in this cloak of shadows and scribbling to midnight. I was completely content. Nothing could threaten the glow of satisfaction that I felt.

This evening, I could hear the river that flowed between our house and my parents. It was not much of a river for most of the year, but after heavy rain it overflowed and became part of a web of streams that flooded the fields and turned the hidden springs and wells into living mouths that gurgled all night. I had never been afraid of this landscape; even though it had once been overrun by IRA men and British soldiers; even in the darkness and knowing all that was hidden there, further up the mountain, where lights winked at other lights, the homes of our neighbours surrounded by thickets of gorse and blackthorn, metaphors for the guarded and wayward men and women who were born there and the contrary paths they had followed. I was going to write a story about the complicated things that had happened between my family and theirs, things of historic gravity, a story full of purpose and without fear, a story that had lain frozen in my parish for years but was now flowing into me like water and brimming over with the truth. I no longer felt afraid of the cycles of history, or of my neighbours who had been living among half-truths for years.

I could feel the story flowing and lifting me higher, threatening to throw me into all sorts of conversations and encounters with people who had been carrying the dead weight of secrets for years.

1982

From the overheated closet, Alice heard one of the gunmen's voices call her maiden name. She was reluctant to move from her hiding place but when her name was repeated in a voice that sounded oddly familiar, she forced herself to open the door a chink. A man stood at the other end of the corridor, hooded in a balaclava, and talking to her husband, Dermot, who was still dressed in his pyjamas. The lob-sided hole in the gunman's mask made it look as though he was grinning hideously.

The mention of her old name gave her a giddy sense of conviction that the paramilitary was a neighbour, and what was happening had something to do with her grandfather and the past. Four more gunmen stood beside the houseplants in the hall. She opened the door, clambered from her hiding-place, and walked down the corridor. Her children piled out after her, a bank of blankets and sheets falling with them. The mass of laundry half buried them, and they had to push their way out of the closet.

The gunman turned away from her husband, his eyes as unblinking as a bird of prey's, and led Alice into the living room, all the time speaking calmly and with a sense of righteousness. He informed her that he was the commander of a group of IRA volunteers, who, in the name of the Irish people, were seizing her car in a military operation against the British forces. He invoked the Easter Rising and its leaders, speaking as if he were teaching a history lesson. She was shocked at the thought of their ten-year-old Renault being commandeered in the fight for Irish freedom.

Another gunman led her husband and children into the room and together the family sat on the sofa and armchairs. The IRA leader went to the side of the window and looked out along the road. An innocent spring morning brightened outside, but in the cramped living room a twisted notion of history reigned. In the hall, the gunmen lit cigarettes. One of them grew jittery and kept tapping his right foot, his fingertips playing lightly along the barrel of his gun. When Alice stared at them, they looked right through her, without any signs of recognition. They were no longer neighbours. They were clad in the paramilitary uniform of the IRA, masks, gloves, black boots, denim jackets and jeans.

The leader kept them confined to the living room. He pulled back the curtains but forbid the children to look out. There he remained, his attention fixed upon a solitary tree on the horizon. He glowered at the landscape and waited. Nothing happened for over an hour. It seemed as though the IRA men were waiting for some sort of message. The silence became unnerving.

Then, the leader announced, "Okay, let's get going." His eyes sparkled and glistened as he bent down and handed the eldest child a bullet. He spoke in a fierce whisper. "That's for you daddy if he rings the police before one o'clock." Then they left in a hurry, forgetting to close the door behind them, as if they had wasted enough time already and could no longer neglect the important job they had to do. They clambered into the Renault and sped away without once looking back.

Alice and Dermot watched from the living room window as the car turned the corner and headed towards the main road. It vanished behind a screen of trees, reappeared, and then was gone for good. She felt like saying something but was unable to find the words. From a corner of the living room, their eleven-year-old son stared at his father. He still held the bullet in his hands. Gently, she took it from him, wrapped it in an old sweetie wrapper and stuffed it down the back of the sofa. She was not thinking straight.

When the couple switched on the one o'clock news, they saw pictures of their car abandoned at the side of a road, doors hanging open, the vehicle partially burnt out but still recognisable. The newsreader described how an IRA gang had used the car to kill an off-duty policeman on a quiet country road in County Armagh. Not a military operation, as the IRA leader had promised, but murder. Alice and Dermot sat hypnotised by the images. Already, they had seen and heard too much.

Mechanically, Dermot reached over and switched it off. He picked up the telephone and rang the police, while Alice wrung her hands, and then, joining them together, prayed for the murdered man and his family. In grave tones, Dermot gave his name and address. Afterwards, they sat together and stared through the living room window, waiting for the arrival of the police.

They were the parents of five children. They were used to the habit of bearing things and obeying the power of fate. They sat in the same positions for a long time, feeling guilty and vulnerable, unable to return to their normal routine, transfixed by the sight of their car on the television. The images resembled the closing shots in a film of their family life and all the journeys they had undertaken in the vehicle. The scenes of its final bloody journey grew like cancer cells, multiplying and devouring their happy memories of summer trips to the beach and visits to relatives.

A British Army helicopter swept low over the hill in

the half-light, and hovered near their house, its rotor blades flashing like lances. The glass in the living room window trembled slightly.

"What shall we tell them about the hijackers?"

The landscape seemed to grow predatory with the helicopter swooping above, the rough hills and humped fields gathering closer as the light faded. Rain fell, thickening the shadows.

Alice turned to check the children weren't listening. "Do we have to say anything?"

"Of course. We have to tell them everything we know."

"Why don't we tell them they were complete strangers? We'll say their faces were hidden behind their masks, and we didn't recognise their voices."

He looked at her. He didn't understand her plea for secrecy. They hadn't done anything wrong. They were the victims in this war between the IRA and the British security forces. She was probably still in shock.

The darkness of the morning still held sway in the hedgerows, which, in their imaginations, had switched to the side of the IRA. The gunmen were now part of the landscape's otherworldly presence; changelings with the power to emerge from the archways of thorn thickets and stride into farmhouses and bungalows, leaving death and destruction in their wake.

The police arrived in the evening. For the second time that day, the family home was invaded. Soldiers stood outside the house, and along the road, checking the passing cars. Like miserable puppets, Alice and Dermot repeated the lines the IRA had told them. The detectives wore faces like stone and interrogated the couple. What exactly did the IRA men say? How did they behave? Could they see their features? They frowned if the couple hesitated. The heart of the morning, the hijackers standing with their guns and announcing their intentions, was hard for Dermot and Alice to recall. They remembered the little details, as in a dream; they knew only that it happened in their home, in front of their children.

A female detective talked to the children and heard the story about the bullet given to the eldest boy. However, Alice was unable to remember what she had done with the bullet. She searched and searched but could not find it anywhere. Scene of crime officers arrived and swept through the house and the hedge at the back of the garden.

The Renault was no longer their family car. It was an instrument of death. For a week, the police impounded and forensically examined it, dusted it for fingerprints and searched it for clues. Officers pawed through the detritus of family life, the sticky ice-lolly wrappers, the cigarette butts in the ashtray, the lines of sand from Donegal beaches. One day, they phoned Dermot and asked him to remove it from the police station. He arranged for it to be towed to his mother's house in County Monaghan, over the border.

The hijacking cast a shadow over the family, a shadow that grew into sinister shapes every night controlled and manipulated by the IRA. The shadow placed them at the mercy of the British Army with its random checkpoints, foot patrols and house raids. They were stopped more often on the roads, made to stand at the side of the second-hand van they were using as a family car while soldiers searched the vehicle and casually called them by their first names. They seemed to know a lot about the couple. Some of the police and soldiers were openly hostile to them, while others were suspicious but polite.

Alice and Dermot wondered how the secret bureaucracy of the British Intelligence Forces had classified them. Had they made a distinction for the couple as victims? Or had they branded them as collaborators and IRA sympathizers? The young soldiers that harassed them didn't seem to understand the difference. One of them leaned through the van window and asked Dermot did he feel safe sleeping in his bed at night.

Dermot became oppressed by the fear that loyalist paramilitaries would target him in a reprisal attack, while in Alice's mind old suspicions of neighbours rose to the surface. She tried to figure out why the IRA had targeted her family, and not her neighbours. She wondered what grievances had pitted her family against the IRA clans, what fates and blood had been mixed in the past and used like weapons against her.

Their phone began ringing at odd hours. When Dermot or Alice answered it, there was the sound of heavy breathing and then a click and they were left with an empty telephone in their hands. The barking of neighbours' dogs and the sudden rumble of tyres on the road kept them awake at night. It occurred to Dermot that they should buy a guard-dog.

One night, their sleep was disturbed by the honking of car horns, engines revving in their driveway, and young men cursing and shouting, "Informers out!" Later, Dermot jerked awake with a gasp, sweat bursting on his forehead. He could still hear the shouts echoing in the darkness, but their tormentors had gone, and a thick silence pressed down upon him. He felt the hatred and suspicion of his neighbours crawl through the silence to where he lay sprawled beside his sleeping wife. He had no idea that such feelings lay hidden in the roots of the parish and in the blood of its young men, waiting for a violent act to bring them forth. Their insults and humiliations churned in his stomach. The parish of Diseart with its whitethorn hedged fields and clear running rivers had seemed so innocent when he first arrived, but he had only looked at the landscape through the frame of love, and his gaze had not been penetrating or direct enough. He began to suspect there was more bloodthirstiness lurking in the border parishes of the North than in the cowboy films he watched as a boy in Monaghan cinemas. It was his bad fortune to set up home in one of the most vengeful, a mountainside full of IRA men and their sympathisers.

Since moving to Diseart, he had tried his best to blend into the background, working as a carpenter on local building sites and helping farming neighbours with their hay and potato harvests. He didn't drink in the local pubs or support the parish GAA team. He slipped into the back of the church on Sundays and left without getting caught up in conversation. He wasn't predisposed to small talk. He was the epitome of modesty and discretion. He passed the first dozen years of his married life without drawing much attention to himself, as clean living as a monk, not smoking or drinking, or betting on horses. Even his father-in-law repeatedly reminded his wife that she had married a good and decent man, about whom nobody could say a bad word.

Now, when he drove to church and listened to the conversations of his neighbours, he noticed how their Tyrone accents sounded thick and sinister. They treated him with elaborate reserve at the gates, nodding politely as he passed, but a vague suspicion hung in the air. Other neighbours didn't respond at all and stole sneaking glances at him.

For three nights in a row, the shouts and curses woke the couple from their sleep. A car drove up to their bedroom window and the sound of its horn filled the night along with voices, shrill, grating voices that shouted taunts and 'yee-haws'. Unable to bear it any longer, Dermot opened the window and roared, "We know who you are." However, the howling grew louder. Alice joined him at the window and tried to calm him down, but he kept shouting, shaken, as though she were one of the enemies. She begged him to come back to bed. She told him the police investigation would collapse, and all this would soon be over. Eventually, their tormentors would stop calling in the middle of the night.

"You're wrong," he said. "This will never be over. It's only just beginning."

2019

We were gathered in a tin-roofed byre, my neighbours and I, watching heavy rain sweeping down the mountain and blurring the little valley below. Some of us carried white envelopes with prayers inside. We smiled, nodded at each other, and kept a certain distance. We breathed the mountain air and listened to the echoing patter of rain, while the two stewards, who had brought us here, stood at the far end of the byre, smoking and glancing over from time to time. With their solemn expressions, high-visibility vests and torches, they resembled guards waiting to go off duty.

More neighbours arrived, and for a while, the interior of the byre grew animated with the murmur of voices. Then the silence returned, and we stood like shadows. An older steward, the one who had directed us to the byre, appeared, and after a whispered consultation with the other two, picked up a bunch of vehicle keys and beckoned us to follow. A minibus sat in the yard, its bulk obscuring the last of the light, and we clambered inside. The door slid shut behind us with a definitive sound. The engine started and the windscreen wipers swept back and forth, even though the rain had stopped. Gears strained and tyres skidded in the mud. Our submissive mood deepened as the vehicle rolled up a lane. We were travelling to the farmhouse of a dead neighbour to pay our respects. We were mourners being ferried to a funeral wake, hushed and respectful, carrying the scent of the living on our skins.

The narrowness of the mountain roads, and the number

of visitors expected to descend from all corners of Tyrone had prompted the local GAA club to post stewards at various points on the approach roads. They directed traffic to a neighbour's farmyard where there was ample parking on a gently sloping field, and a fleet of minibuses and jeeps waiting to transport the mourners. As it was, cars were parked mindlessly along the lanes, wedged up at gate entrances, passing places, and grassy banks as though they had climbed up to escape a great flood.

We could see a river of mourners at the front of the wake house. Another line of people milled from a side door. It was December, the darkest time of the year, and a cold wind scoured the mountainside of gorse and blackthorn hedges. The hall of the house turned out to be as cramped as the inside of the minibus. I said my name amid a thicket of low voices and shook hands with the dead man's eldest son, who led me into a room that lay completely empty apart from the corpse and the grieving wife. The son introduced me as the local journalist and mentioned the name of the newspaper I had once worked for. I offered her my hand and said my condolences. She held onto it, in the way people hold onto hands at a time of death, and gazed at me, as if waiting for more words.

"You write for the paper?"

"Yes," I replied semi-apologetically, even though it had been more than a year since my by-line had appeared in it.

The grown-up sons and daughters talked the entire time without stopping for breath. They chatted amiably about ordinary little things that had happened in the days leading up to their father's death, repeating the same stories. I had been in that same position, after the death of my youngest brother, Paul, in a room glowing with candles, feeling overwhelmed as I watched the constant stream of visitors winding slowly around the coffin, the names and faces changing constantly, as in a dream. What did I feel during that first night of mourning for my little brother, when the wake was in full swing, and the swarming shadows of my neighbours surrounded me resolutely, shaking my hand and offering condolences? A grief that surpassed and transformed itself and any individual feeling of sadness, the expression of it growing into something precise and finely honed as the night wore on. I saw the restraint in my neighbours' faces as their eyes riveted on my brother's youthful face, and when I shook their hands, the depths in each one of them opened before me into a bottomless sea of sorrow.

I remembered this as I walked around the coffin. The wake's symbolic power exerted a force that could not be resisted and was completely different to the aura around a funeral service, where the words and rituals were often difficult to connect with reality. A wake, on the other hand, was an expression of longing, a community binding itself through the primordial force of death, and the way it did this was through constant chatting, leaving no room for death to say anything.

But I was unable to say anything. I was tongue-tied, worried that I might forget the names of the grieving sons and daughters or ignore completely a bereaved relative. A young woman handed me a cup of tea, and another presented a tray of sandwiches and buns. I drifted out of the bedroom and into the kitchen. Death turned lives upside down, but in the wake house, everything was orderly and calm, the tables filled with neatly cut sandwiches. Women methodically replenished cups of tea. Any sign of havoc or mess had been tidied away.

It struck me that there were two types of grief, one that was tied to a place, and another that was not. When you lived in a parish with people you had grown up and gone to school with, it was impossible to turn your back on a neighbour's sorrow or look the other way. We knew each other's parents and grandparents and could trace our family connections back for over a hundred years. But what were the things we had turned away from, the intimate secrets and little quirks we ignored in each other? Straight away, in the sitting room, I spotted Malachy Warde, an ex-IRA man. His pointed face, with its expression of concentration, made everyone entering the room look at him first. Even though he was from another parish, everyone knew him because of his paramilitary past and his several spells in jail. His eyes were pale, very pale green. They seemed to see through everything, through the drama of bereavement, the circus of parish life, and the gossiping of the mourners.

He had his usual place at wakes, in a comfortable armchair in the main room, seated amid the throng, but maintaining an air of separation, with the rigidity of a man wearing a blindfold. Every now and again, he talked quietly to a passing neighbour. His conversation could not be overheard and always seemed distinct and separate from the words of consolation and small talk exchanged by everyone else. Whenever I looked in his direction, just a fleeting glimpse, he turned and stared at me with his piercing eyes. As a teenager, I had always squirmed in his gaze, like a rat cornered by a hunting dog. Each time I met him, my mind was reluctant to draw on the memories of the IRA hijacking. My family had suffered an injustice at the hands of his comrades, a violent act, but memories faded over time, or were filtered unconsciously. I preferred to dwell on the times that I had seen him diligently picking up his grandchildren on the school-run or collecting money for third-world charities, the quiet interludes of his career as an IRA man. Instinctively, I skipped over the thought of him crouching in a hedge and wielding a gun.

Warde was no longer carrying guns or holding families hostage, but, through his gaze, he was still setting traps for his neighbours. I watched him stir his cup of tea with a spoon and lift it to his lips: the same movement of his hand and arm that had once lifted and fired a gun and was now being blessed by the hospitality of a grieving family. He had recruited the innocent spoon and white china cup to prove that he was here as a respected friend and neighbour, not an enemy. He was seeking validation for the violent laws he had lived by as a young man. He had succeeded in protecting the parish from loyalist paramilitaries and British soldiers. He was one of the good guys, and the bad guys, our enemies, lay outside the parish, not within it. That was the message in his green eyes, and if the china cup and spoon were to waltz around the room under the force of his gaze, they would have repeated the same message. All the unexpected cruelties of the IRA campaign, the hijackings and intimidations of Catholic neighbours, they were someone else's oversights or errors.

His eyes blazed in the centre of the room, getting as close to his neighbours as he could, checking how secret were the things that needed to be kept secret, the sea of hidden crimes that with each passing year seemed to grow murkier and higher, implicating everyone in parishes like ours who had looked the other way, who saw and knew what the IRA were doing, but pretended not to see or know. It struck me that if I were to write a book about how the Troubles flowed through my parish it would have to include him as a character. I would have to trap the reader in his thoughts, in his point-of-view, in that relentless gaze of his.

But was it just his past that drew everyone to him? Shooting people was extreme, blowing them to smithereens was extreme, but Warde was also a good neighbour, a hard-working farmer with a family of seven children, a regular Mass-goer. In their heart of hearts, had men like him always wanted to kill another human being? Walking up the church aisle to receive Holy Communion every Sunday, dropping off his children at football training, checking on his elderly neighbours during the winter, was murder what he really wanted, if he ever got the chance? I didn't think so, but how could I be sure?

Grief in a rural parish meant that families could not close their doors and lower their blinds. Men like Warde could not be shut out physically. Death reminded us that they could not be eliminated or ignored. Even in our most private dwelling places, in the sanctuary of our grief, we had to invite them in, serve them a cup of tea and a sandwich or two, and allow their gaze to fall upon our loved ones. But what else were we submitting ourselves to, what values were we adopting in the system of subtle control that ran through the border parishes of Northern Ireland, and had the potential to be more dystopian than anything inspired by Orwell?

I didn't want to speak to Warde, even though I suspected he might hold the answer to why the IRA had held us at gunpoint and hijacked our car all those years ago. At the very least, he would be able to help me track down the IRA man who had handed me a bullet for my father. Speaking to him, or being seen in his company, had its dangers. He was a living connection to the worst days of the Troubles. He had done things to other human beings that gave him a distinctly powerful aura and isolated him from his neighbours just as much as the dead man in the coffin lay separated from the living. And, anyway, if I were to ask him about the hijacking, how would I get round to the subject? How would I force myself to approach him in the first place?

I watched the way he ostentatiously greeted everyone who passed by his chair, and the restrained reverence of the other mourners around him. He craned his neck, surveying the line of visitors, turning his head with a jerky movement. A pair of hands holding a teapot replenished his cup. He sipped the tea, but his single-minded gaze remained vigilant.

He glanced across the room and caught me staring at him. I looked away and when my eyes flicked back, he was still watching me. He nodded, grinned and waited for my response. I nodded back, and then he got up and came over.

"Let's go somewhere we can talk," he muttered, passing close by me like a man who had the right to summon whomever he wanted from the room.

I wanted to leave anyway. I followed him into the hall, out the back door and into the night, feeling as though my life was turning into a series of events elicited by the story I wanted to write, one event prompting another: Loughderg and my mother, and now this wake and an ex-IRA man.

The back of the farmhouse extended farther than I imagined, leading through a small maze of outhouses and concrete yards, all deserted in the moonlight. We emerged onto a manure-strewn yard surrounded by empty cattle-stalls. Some sort of winch stood mounted on a metal base with a taut cable stretching into the darkness. I felt uncomfortable and hung back.

"One of his cows fell into the slurry pit," explained

Warde. "They were trying to haul it out when he took a heart attack."

I nodded. Somewhere nearby lay a subterranean cistern full of rotting manure and urine.

"Poor man, he almost fell in with the bloody cow." Warde watched me carefully. "Quite a crowd here," he added. Only his eyes moved. He cleared his throat and frowned. I realised he was going to say something completely unrelated to the farmer's death.

"I want to talk to you about a story," he announced.

A fearful instinct kicked in. For a moment, I believed he had taken offence at a story I'd published. "One that I've written?" I asked. My face must have turned grey in the moonlight. Had I been hauled to the edge of this cesspit as a form of warning?

"No," he said, grinning. "One that I want you to write."

He explained that a few months previously, workmen renovating a house near Blackwatertown had discovered a gun wrapped up in rags under the floorboards with a bag containing bullets and two instruction manuals. The workmen had immediately phoned the police, who came and removed the weapon, and everything found with it. Warde believed that the gun had been a personal protection firearm issued to a serving police officer whose identity was being kept secret. The gun, he suspected, was one of the weapons used by loyalist killers during the 1970s in a series of murders of Catholics that had earned that corner of Armagh and Tyrone the grim title of The Murder Triangle.

"What do you want me to do?" I said.

"Ask questions. Get the police to set the record straight. The house belonged to a man called Clive Adams in the mid-1970s. Ring any bells?"

"No."

"He's dead now, but he was a convicted member of the gang linked to the Murder Triangle."

"How many killings are we talking about?"

"Dozens."

Was it the moonlight, my imagination, or a combination of both? A silky menace had taken hold of his face. "We've got the police on the run," he declared. "They can't hide from the truth anymore."

I knew the details of the Murder Triangle had been dug over to death, that so many facts had been repressed or distorted that the investigating authorities no longer knew what the truth was and what was a cover-up. Several times, the police and the justice system had tried to draw a line under it, claiming there was no evidence of official collusion between the police and loyalist paramilitaries. Warde fed me the same story I had heard countless times, whispering in his cold, precise way. How Catholic representatives like Father Denis Faul had drawn the patterns out of the darkness by a mixture of instinct and deduction - the invisible set of connections that lay just beneath the surface of the murders.

Father Faul had published his findings in a pamphlet called 'The Triangle of Death'. He wrote about the size and number of the bullets fired, the descriptions of the strike marks, the entry points on the victims' bodies, the getaway cars and the statements of eyewitnesses, some of whom reported seeing police checkpoints near the shootings. Along with others, Faul compiled the names of the men charged with minor roles in the killings, some of whom were listed as ex-police officers. With a little more digging, it emerged that the men had been in the police service at the time of their involvement in the murders and had resigned from the force on the day of their trials. What

Faul and the other researchers lacked were the details of the murder weapon itself.

Eventually, they obtained a confidential police report showing that the gun used in the attacks was a Spanish made Star pistol. It was impossible not to agree with the priest's conclusion. When a weapon was used in a similar type of attack, in a similar area and at around the same time, it suggested the attacks were linked, if not committed by the same people. The murders were not a series of random sectarian attacks, as the authorities were making out, but a concerted campaign of murder.

But, even if Warde had a new lead and an interesting story at the heart of it, why should he think I would write it? His presumption made me feel apprehensive. At the same time, I felt annoyed because he had touched on my own unfulfilled ambition of writing a story about the Troubles. He had given voice to my yearnings. I glanced at his eyes. Had his special gaze sensed that I had come to the wake like a spy, searching for a way to begin my story about my grandfather and the IRA man who had handed me a bullet, searching for something that my neighbours might know and I did not? I had discovered a secret story of my own, and I needed to pose important questions to people like Warde. It occurred to me that researching his story might allow me a circular path to the story I really wanted to write. He would think he was leading me, but in fact, I would be leading him, and out of his story, something original and unexpected might be created.

"What are you thinking?" he asked.

I blinked, marshalled my thoughts, and tried to work out what I should say, and what I should conceal, which role I should play, and which I should disguise.

"Why come to me?"

"You wrote a book about the Murder Triangle."

"Yes. It was called *Silence*. But it was a work of fiction. A crime novel."

"The relatives of the victims didn't think so. They said they could work out who exactly you were writing about. They said you got the truth dead right."

"I never set out to tell the truth about the Murder Triangle. I just wanted to tell a story."

He looked at me blankly. He seemed unsure of the distinction I had made. I held my tongue. I wanted to tell him that a work of fiction tells many stories, but a work of truth and facts only one, that facts can be arranged and told in ways that might hint at an elusive truth, and that even a crime novel could hide a secret tale. However, I didn't want to add to the haughty and ignorant look on his face. This wasn't a discussion on metafiction, and Warde wasn't a creative writing student. Besides, I wasn't sure if I believed in that old horseshit anymore.

I fell back on the stock response I gave to outlandish writing requests. "I don't think I can. It's not the sort of story I do."

"What sort of story do you do?"

I hesitated.

"You're happy for the police to cover this up?" His eyes widened.

My book about the Murder Triangle wasn't the only reason we were having this conversation, I realised. I belonged to a parish the IRA once controlled with violence and intimidation, and in some fundamental way, he thought he could still control me.

"It's time all the details of the murder triangle were cleared up," he said. "Everyone guilty held to account."

"And who's everyone?"

"The killers, the men who pulled the strings in the background and their messengers. The police and the judiciary, too."

I raised an eyebrow.

"Look, the police think they're the winners," he said. "They're refusing to hang their dirty laundry in public. We need to tell the story before the gun vanishes for good."

"I have to go."

"Wait. I'm just asking you to help us. All you have to do is ring the police press office, do some digging. Get a simple statement of fact from them, something to acknowledge they have the gun. You're a journalist. This will put the wind up them."

But I was no longer a well-connected journalist, or any type of journalist. It had been months since the discovery of the gun, if it had ever occurred in the first place. A police press officer might find it too difficult to track down the details now.

"Look," added Warde. "Think of the victims' families. They're at the end of their rope. They want this out in the open and explained. The last thing they want is to be kept in the dark with all sorts of suspicions festering. One of their solicitors contacted the police but he got nowhere. They denied any knowledge of the gun. The thought of another cover-up is putting the families through hell."

His tone sounded more distracted than confrontational, and I realised that he was pleading with me to write the story, not threatening me.

"I understand."

I stared at the winch. But, at the same time, he was trying to use me. This was all part of a propaganda war, a way to undermine the reputation of the new police service. The silence about the gun wasn't right, but in the context of the Troubles what was? The police might never release any details about the weapon, leaving the families in a cloud of suspicion and ignorance.

"Just a quick phone call."

A quick phone call.

"Mention that the relatives know about the gun and want answers."

Just a quick phone call, one that might be ignored completely or given a stock response to by the police about an ongoing investigation. If what Warde was saying was true, then the police had questions to answer, explosive questions that would have to be answered quickly in order to reassure the victims' families that the authorities were dedicated to upholding justice and the truth. What had the police done with the weapon? Had it been examined forensically? Had its details been passed to the Historical Enquiries Team? Why had there been a delay in reporting its finding to the press?

"One more thing," said Warde. "The UVF tried to kill my son with that gun. They riddled our living room with bullets one night. I've an account I want to settle with it." His voice was soft, a little husky. At the same time, he was excited, which told me something about the emotions the discovery of such a weapon would stir. He wanted the blame placed on the police, to have them covered in the blood drawn by the gun. He wanted to prove that the police were complicit, had crossed the line, and might do so again. His breathing turned hoarse and greedy. He talked about the gun as if men had not done the shooting and killing, as if the weapon had somehow possessed a cold will of its own, marching from house to house across the darkened countryside of Tyrone and Armagh. Shadowy men had held the gun, but they had somehow been subordinate to its role, secondary partners in its grim dance. Was that the notion all killers clung to? I wondered.

Weapons held the ultimate power, the power over life, and not their human handlers. The weapon was the killer, literally and figuratively, and hence the emotion in his voice.

"What are the families hoping to get out of this?"

"Everything. Ballistics, names, dates, places. The whole story of the Murder Triangle."

I wanted to ask what was in it for him. Was it the truth or something darker, a piece of propaganda to divert attention from other crimes closer to home?

"Unless journalists start asking questions the gun will disappear or be accidentally destroyed," he said.

But this wasn't a simple request or a run-of-the-mill story that would turn into a self-contained report in a local newspaper. A sense of urgency and danger emanated from the discovery of the gun. It overflowed with troubling questions and hinted at deeper meanings. It spoke of the grey areas of collusion and ambiguous truth. But hadn't IRA men like Warde played an active part in creating this grey area, grinding their god-fearing neighbours into submission and cooperation, oppressing them with threats of violence. Didn't the greatest fault lie with the men and women on both sides who had murdered and maimed?

What good will this do? I wanted to ask him. All this searching for connections and conspiracies. How would it really help the families of the victims? Or anyone for that matter? What difference would it make to their lives, knowing which weapon had killed their loved ones? The men who had done the killing were in their graves and had taken their secrets with them. They were beyond justice. But somehow, the weapon was not.

A wind picked up, agitating the trees and blackthorn bushes, multiplying the pattern of shadows that fell across the concrete yard. Their restless movement made Warde's eyes seem calm and eerily stable.

"What if the police officer issued this weapon is still in the force?" asked Warde. "Perhaps in a high-ranking role?"

And what if the police officer had been the victim of coercion or the weapon stolen from him? A resident of a loyalist area ruled by fear and intimidation. Who was Warde to point the finger of blame, or rush to moral judgement? We tell our stories, bury our dead, get on with our lives and try to build a better future for our children, forgetting that in parishes like ours the Troubles had yet to end. We were walled in by the past, and beyond those walls shadowy men still roamed, tidying up a bloody legacy.

"I'll see what I can do," I said.

He nodded, turned on his heel and stalked back to the house.

A woman's voice sounded in the night. "Who were you talking to?"

"A journalist. One of ours."

I walked away as fast as possible. The story I was going to write was no longer mine. It was his. Somehow, I had missed the moment of the switch. And now his story's alien shadow would follow me around, dogging me with questions and suspicions.

1982

Dermot woke up, feeling that someone had entered the bedroom. He thought it was one of the IRA men. For several moments, he was convinced the gunmen had never left their home and his family were still being held hostage. Somehow, he and Alice had forgotten or overlooked the fact that the IRA had taken up permanent residence in their living room. Then he remembered that the IRA gunmen had killed a man and had already accomplished their mission. For a while, he hovered between the world of dreams and the waking world, a half-awake eye on both.

Even on nights like these when their tormentors didn't call, Dermot could still imagine the blazing headlights of the cars flashing across the ceiling and hear their shouts of abuse. Fully awake now, he looked at Alice, lying asleep beside him. What did she know about their IRA neighbours, this underside to parish life? He would never know what she knew because he was an outsider and would always lead an outsider's life. The hijacking had been a monstrous invasion of his household, but to her it seemed something else, a sad confirmation of old truths shared between neighbours. This was the real damage in all this trouble. Not to know what she and their neighbours knew. She had told him not to worry, that the intimidation would soon end, but how did she know for sure. Not knowing was the source of his agitation. He loved her and wanted to live with her in Diseart. He'd thought he was settling into the rhythms of life here, but every time he closed his eyes, he felt as though he were plunging headfirst into darkness.

He brushed against her and wondered if she would awake. He wanted her to be conscious, lying with him in the darkness, listening and alert, but she barely stirred. She seemed locked away in a less troubled world. Had her dreams been arranged so that they too would hide secrets?

He rose in the pitch darkness, pulled on a cold shirt and a pair of trousers. Barefoot, he walked quietly from the bedroom into the kitchen. He opened the back door and stared into the starlit night, watching and waiting for the IRA to make their next move. Everything was silent. The darkness and the thorn hedges waited, too. Perhaps his tormentors had to go somewhere else tonight or had been delayed. They had chosen another family to harass, or they were deciding to kill again, chatting in low voices in a back room somewhere, having a smoke and a final glass of whiskey or poteen.

Ever since the hijacking, his senses and reflexes had started living a new life, and at night the shadowy view of hills and fields from his backdoor seemed like the strangest country he had ever seen. He stood at the door for a long time, his eyes adjusting to the dim light. Something was watching him silently from the slowly expanding darkness, something not necessarily human or even animal, a gun barrel, a pair of binoculars or a security force camera whirring and clicking.

"Is that you, Dermot?" said a voice behind him. Barefoot and noiseless, his wife was standing in the kitchen.

"Yes, it's me."

"Can't you sleep?"

"No. You know I can't."

She took hold of his hand, intertwining her fingers with his.

"Are you afraid?"

"No, I'm not."

Beyond this brief exchange in the middle of the night, they barely discussed the threat that loomed over their lives. The next day, Dermot phoned the police and reported the night-time harassment. The detective who came on the line explained the police were eager to help, but first their persecutors had to make a specific threat to harm them. Nevertheless, the detective recorded the incident on a file and asked them to keep a record of the harassment. Neither Dermot nor Alice said anything more about what was happening with the police investigation, the IRA intimidation, the ramifications of the hijacking. They were the parents of five young children, trapped in the throes of running a household and earning a living.

One night, a new detective arrived at their back door, dressed in a black tie that fluttered in the wind, and a long brown raincoat. His appearance, crashing in on the family's evening meal, felt sinister. There was a sad expression on his face, and he introduced himself as Detective Brian Murphy. He shook Dermot's hand. "It's been a while, Dermot," he said. "We have some catching up to do." Despite his sad expression, he smiled warmly.

It turned out that Dermot knew the detective from childhood. They had gone to school together, sometimes playing at break-times, but he had almost forgotten Murphy and had heard only vague rumours that he had joined the police force. The boy Dermot remembered as Brian Murphy belonged to his old world, but, somehow, in one bold stroke, he had turned into a detective. He had stepped into this other world that Dermot shared with his young family and from which he felt secretly estranged. No one else from his old world had ever appeared on his threshold in such a manner. Murphy had not forgotten him, or their schooldays, and was able to recall some classroom incidents with great accuracy. For a while, they talked about their old headteacher, who drove a black Ford Austin and used to send the boys with a can to get petrol. Murphy hesitated and said he would like to call back some evening for another chat, if that was okay. He was no longer sad looking. In fact, he seemed cheery and in good spirits. Dermot nodded.

"Sorry to bother you," said Murphy before leaving.

Dermot shook his hand again. "No bother, at all."

However, when the detective had left, he went over their conversation in his head and pondered Murphy's use of the word 'chat'. He worried that the police had set some sort of trap for him. He suspected they had sent Murphy to gain his trust and wheedle more information from him. Nevertheless, he was glad that an old school friend might now be working on the case.

When Murphy called again, a few nights later, he was wearing the same warm smile and shook Dermot's hand. He asked about Alice and the children. He kept his smile trained on Dermot. This time, he had a folder of photographs with him. He asked Dermot did he recognise any of the men from the morning of the hijacking. Dermot made it clear that he and his wife had no idea who the IRA men were. Murphy placed the photographs on the table, but Dermot refused to look at them.

In the days that followed, Murphy began calling unexpectedly, sometimes with a female colleague, sometimes alone. Alice made him wait at the front door while she called for Dermot, who usually stood in the porch and talked to the detective. Most of the time their conversations were short and to the point, Murphy delivering the latest update on the investigation.

Late one night, he turned up with a car full of police officers and told Dermot that the IRA gang had struck again, holding another family hostage, and hijacking their car. This time, he was specific in what he wanted from Dermot. All he needed was a description of the hijackers and an eyewitness testimony. Did any of them have a ginger beard showing through their masks? What height and shape were they? Did he recognise their voices?

"You and your neighbours know who these men are," he told Dermot. He showed him four mugshots, and then several more sets of the same faces. "Unless they're stopped, they'll kill again," he warned.

Dermot stared at the photographs and shook his head while Alice placed the kettle on the gas hob. Slowly, the kettle began to hiss. Murphy expressed his concern and sympathy once again for Alice and the children. He asked about their emotional states. He said his calls to their house were meant as a show of support. He praised the couple for coping so courageously with the intimidation from their neighbours. However, as one of the detectives assigned to the case, he had to see the investigation through to the end. He didn't want to say anything more, but, in the circumstances, he couldn't help confiding that the police now knew with certainty who the hijackers were and had placed them under surveillance. In fact, they were hoping to arrest them soon under the Prevention of Terrorism act. He apologised for bringing it up, but the prosecutors were concerned they might have to release the suspects without charge if new evidence did not emerge.

"If you're feeling up to it," said Murphy, "I'd really like you and Alice to keep these photographs and study them. I don't need you to formally identify them. Just tell me whatever you feel comfortable with."

The detective's gaze was long and cool. He waited. Dermot looked at the photographs and said nothing, while Alice glanced over his shoulder.

"No, we can't," said Dermot and pushed the photographs back towards Murphy. The kettle whistled with steam, but Alice did not remove it from the hob. Its shrill noise filled the kitchen.

2019

When ex-police detective Gregory Daley and his wife, Sarah, arrived at my parent's house, fresh off the overnight plane from New York, my mother had laid on such a profusion for them, home-made Irish breads, cakes and a cooked breakfast, and also mementoes from the past, photographs, letters, household implements and tools from the early 20th Century, all sorts of memorabilia from her father's life, arranged on a side-table in the sitting room. Gregory was one of her newly discovered US relatives, the son of Samuel Daley, whom her American granduncle, Patrick Daly, had adopted during the First World War. My mother never did anything half-heartedly, and her welcome for this stranger, who was not even a blood relative, was no exception.

Patrick Daly was my grandfather's uncle, and I'd heard a few sketchy details about him. According to the family legend, he'd found wealth investing in railway stock in America, and had married but was childless. Not long after the Donaghy murder, he'd written a letter to his sister, declaring his wish to adopt his nephew, my grandfather, and bring him to a better life in the US. Unfortunately, Patrick had been travelling to New York in the autumn of 1918 to get the boat back to Ireland when he was killed in a notorious railway accident. My mother's father never mentioned him until one day she found a large, framed photograph of him covered in dust in her grandmother's back room. Of all the family stories she had heard, she was most intrigued by Patrick's, and for years afterwards, she was captivated by the over-exposed photograph and the ghostly smoothness of Patrick's face, this strange relative who had come to rescue her grandfather from poverty but had tragically died on the journey. However, no other trace of Patrick remained, not even a last address or a burial place, and his memory survived as one of those tall stories every family possesses, the wealthy connection in the New World lost to time and the twists of fate.

Through DNA and ancestry research, my mother and my sister, Patricia, discovered many lost relatives online, most of them in the US and Canada. Some had taken my mother by surprise, leading her down unknown avenues in her family's past. In some cases, the links were so obscure that I suspected her newly discovered ancestry was as much a product of fantasy and projection as of careful research and fact checking. One of the most surprising discoveries that had floated up out of their internet searches was a passport with a picture of Patrick Daly, the same ghostly photograph in the frame that had gathered dust in her granny's back room. The US government had issued the passport in 1918, the year Patrick had undertaken his ill-fated journey to Ireland. He must have applied for the passport in order to make the sea crossing and sent a copy of the photograph to his family in Ireland in advance, probably with the letter declaring his intention to adopt his nephew. To my mother and sister's excitement, the passport mentioned a next of kin, his wife, Catherine, and an address. The story of her granduncle was now anchored to a place: Wantage, Sussex County, New Jersey. Armed with the address, she began to salvage more information about her granduncle. She discovered that he and his wife had adopted a young boy, called Samuel, in 1916, and had not died childless, as the family in Ireland had always believed.

From the comfort of her armchair, she was able to leap over the decades, the Great Depression and the Second World War, and follow Samuel through the census. She found him married in 1952, living in New Orleans, with a daughter called Cathy and a baby son called Gregory. For some reason, he now spelled his surname Daley, rather than Daly. Several more shots at the census revealed that by 1978 Gregory was a police detective, married with two children, and still living in the same district he had been born in, but at a place called Belle Chase. After several trawls through Facebook, my sister sent a message on my mother's behalf to a man they suspected was Gregory Daley, now retired and living in Chalmette. After several months of silence, he responded, confirming the scant details they knew about Samuel. He told them his father had died just a year previously, and he and my mother began sending emails to each other. Some months later, Gregory announced he wanted to pay his respects to the parish that had produced his adoptive grandfather, and announced he was booking flights to Ireland.

Gregory appeared fresh in spite of his long journey from the States. He was in his mid-60s, with silvery hair and a tanned face. He looked well for his age, square and Irish American solid, tough as you'd expect a retired police detective to be. From the moment I first saw him, he had a cigar clenched in his mouth or in his hand. Sarah was younger, blonde-haired and Scandinavian looking, his second wife, we presumed.

"Did you do all this cooking, Alice?" asked Gregory when he stepped into the dining room and saw the spread my mother had arranged for them. His voice was slow, a Southern drawl.

"Yes," she replied.

He and Sarah stood still, staring at the two tables, a

feast for lost travellers, one full of food, the other full of memories and stories.

Gregory's eyes moistened slightly. "You've just about everything here."

They sat down at the table and looked around. My mother's overflowing welcome had a silencing effect on them. A welcome so generous it could have been shared among all her lost relatives. She asked would they like tea or coffee. They took coffee. Gregory placed his cigar in an ashtray and sipped from his cup. He looked down with a furrowed brow, slowly corrected his expression and smiled at my mother. Unfortunately, fresh coffee was the one weak spot in my mother's hospitality skills.

My mother introduced me, and his firm eyes fixed on mine. "So, you're the writer?"

I shook his hand and said yes.

"Your mother sent me your first book," he said. "It's difficult to write books. Not many people can. You've written, how many, nine? That's really something."

I smiled and told him it wasn't that difficult, as long as you kept writing a little every day.

He looked as though he was going to say something else, but then he lowered his gaze. My father's footsteps sounded in the hall. He stuck his head round the door and greeted the guests. He hoped they enjoyed their stay, and then, he excused himself, not wanting to interrupt their discussion on family history. Before retreating, he flashed me a look and quietly closed the door behind him. I knew his opinion on my mother's family tree research – it was a sign of old age, possibly even dotage.

"Come," said my mother to Gregory, "before we eat let me show you what we've got on your grandfather."

She led them to the table of memorabilia. Gregory lit a fresh cigar and contemplated the framed photograph of

Patrick Daly, the passport documents and the birth certificate, and the newspaper article about the railway crash. He stared at the photograph for a long time as though there was something mysterious and moving about it. My mother watched him, waiting for him to make a remark, perhaps a few words about the past, a sentimental reminiscence, but the only comment he made was about the size of the frame in relation to the photograph.

My mother took out a folder of family research. She removed some pages of photocopied pictures and documents and handed them to Gregory.

"I've just two pages about your father Samuel and where he came from," she said.

He nodded, put down his cigar, and began to read them.

"This is fascinating."

"Do you think so?"

"Of course."

"I'll give you more about your grandfather Patrick, later."

He smiled. "I'm sure you will."

I helped my mother serve breakfast, and for the next twenty minutes or so, no one spoke. We ate and clattered our knives and forks. The silence went on for so long that when my mother poured coffee into Gregory's cup, it sounded as though it were spilling into the bottom of a well. The meal ended and Gregory stood up. He said he and his wife were both tired after their long journey.

My mother showed them to the guest bedroom, fussing around them, asking were they warm and comfortable enough, and was there anything else they needed. She encouraged them to use the landline if they wanted to ring home to their family. Her generosity was met by quiet shakes of the head.

"We'll have lunch around one," my mother announced. "Will you be all right until then?"

"Yes."

"I've some day trips planned. And visits to relatives. The O'Briens and the Murphys in Carrickmore would like to meet you, too."

"Oh, right."

"Good, that's settled then."

"I think we'll have a lie-down for a bit, if you don't mind."

"Of course. Let me know if you need anything else."

"Ok. See you later."

My mother was a difficult person to say no to. She got pleasure from caring for others. It was her way of being, and deeply rooted in her childhood. Her greatest fear was that she might end up orphaned and alone in the world. The shadow of her mother's absence fell over her childhood and made her strict in her selfless concern for others, for her father, her patients as a nurse, and her family, too. She could have spoiled herself a little without worrying about the rest of us, but people of her generation did not know how to handle self-indulgence. And now she was welcoming this pair of strangers as though they were long lost messengers bringing good news, a couple who weren't blood relatives at all, whose surname, the one link they had with my mother, was spelled with an extra 'e', as though the name had unravelled slightly, a warning sign from fate.

When the guests had retreated to their bedroom to rest, my mother grabbed me and asked, "Well, what do you think?"

"About what?"

"Our visitors."

I hesitated. "Gregory doesn't seem that keen to talk about family history."

"He's tired from his journey. He'll be ready for some questions later. You'll come up this evening, won't you? Your dad will probably do another disappearing act."

"I'd like to."

"Tomorrow, I'm taking them on a trip around Tyrone. We'll visit all the historical sites. That might help jog Gregory's memory."

"What are you hoping to find out from him?"

It was her turn to hesitate. She would only know when she found it, was what her silence said. Was she looking for stories about the man who might have been her step grandfather, a dream of a life she might have led in the US, if Patrick had taken her father there? Or was it just another connection with the past, a means to cure the lonely child within her? Of all the relatives my mother and sister had tracked down, Gregory occupied the greyest zone. His father, if he were the correct Samuel Daley, had been adopted and bore no blood links, and so their DNA would never clear up the doubt. I saw her uncertainty and remembered that the best stories are those that are full of ambiguity, those with mysteries that can never be solved. My mother had been obsessed by her granduncle and his tragic death, and wanted desperately to hear a fresh story about him, a story that would evoke his life and unite her with him through the living presence of his grandson.

When I joined them at dinner in the evening, the conversation was still restrained. It seemed no one had ever asked Gregory about his grandfather before, and he couldn't remember ever talking to his father about Patrick Daly. Whatever recollections Samuel had of Patrick Daly had been too vague to be termed memories. They had belonged to a twilight vision, unconnected to the rest of his life. As it turned out, Samuel had been a cruel father, an alcoholic to his deathbed, and Gregory's childhood had been an unhappy one. Gregory told my mother he didn't like talking about the past, especially about his father.

"You wouldn't have liked him very much, Alice, if you had met him," he said.

"But he had a hard life," she replied. "Adopted and then left fatherless again when Patrick was killed. He must have been a difficult person to know. Were you sad when he died?"

"Sad?" He stared at my mother in surprise. "All I felt was anger."

"Did he ever mention his childhood?"

"He didn't like that he was adopted." Gregory's gaze grew bleak. "He was ashamed about it. He would never talk about his childhood, even if you begged him. And he was hard on everyone around him. Especially my mother. It was impossible to squeeze anything out of him."

I watched my mother's face, her expression full of eagerness to hear more. However, Gregory clammed up and ate the rest of his meal in silence. Afterwards, he excused himself, and walked into the garden, where he smoked two cigars in quick succession, while Sarah sipped tea with a blank expression. When Gregory returned, my mother rose courteously and asked him did he want some more coffee.

"No, thank you." He frowned.

She began reading from some tourism brochures and gave a running commentary on all the historic sites in Tyrone, glancing over at Gregory to see if anything snagged his interest. She talked about the linen mills in Dungannon and Cookstown, and how the surrounding farmhouses had a weaving or needle room in an outbuilding where the cloth was woven and sewn together.

Gregory leaned forward and looked through the leaflets with interest. "This is intriguing," he said, tapping some of the old photographs. "I remember my father saying how grateful he was that Patrick taught him the skills of tailoring. He was always able to earn money mending clothes."

I looked across at my mother, who had frozen, her hands full of leaflets.

"What skills as a tailor?" she asked quietly. The leaflets hovered in the air.

Patrick Daly had never been a tailor, as far we knew. He had spent his entire life working with trains, earning his wealth from the expansion of railway lines across America.

Gregory began to speak, but then stopped, as if stumbling upon a memory. Surely, he must have known that Patrick Daly was not a tailor. My mother would have told him about the railways. For a moment, he seemed cornered. His brow darkened. Was this it - the truth? My mother had invited over the wrong people, descendants of a different Patrick Daly. Or was there a way out for Gregory and his story? Would he suggest that tailoring had been his grandfather's hobby, or that he had been mistaken, and it was his grandmother who had passed down the sewing skills?

However, Gregory didn't say anything. He must have noticed the look of puzzlement on my mother's face and was trying to think of something to say. We could all feel it, something important hanging in the air, words that were just within reach and on the tip of everyone's tongues, but none of us could summon.

Eventually Gregory spoke. "Oh, they were just some tricks he picked up with a needle, that's all."

My mother let her hand drop. She placed the leaflets on the table.

"What about the railways, did your father ever talk about them?"

"My dad's memory was shot to pieces. He didn't remember that much, only where he'd hidden his whiskey." He laughed with a hint of scorn and his wife gave him a glance. "I might have heard something about the railways," he added. "Yes, I think I did. A lot of the Irish worked on the railways in New Jersey."

"What about your father's old friends? Any of them still alive?"

"Friends?"

"Yes. The people he grew up with, who knew his family. It's possible some of them might remember what Samuel's father did for a living."

"I don't think so," said Gregory. "My father didn't have any old friends. Just the latest set of drinking buddies."

However, my mother was determined to leave no stone unturned.

"Then what about neighbours and acquaintances, former work-mates? Do you have any objection to us trying to hunt down anyone who knew your father's family?"

He stroked his jaw. He glanced at his wife, but she avoided his gaze. It took several moments for him to respond. "No, no objection at all."

The atmosphere became suffocating, but I was unable to leave. It felt as though the past was swallowing us up. Gregory rose and went into the garden again. He stood as stiff as a plank of wood with an unlit cigar in his mouth, while his wife stayed at the table, her face set in stone.

After the first evening, Gregory and Sarah retreated

further into themselves. They had planned to stay with my parents for a week, before completing a quick tour of the Atlantic coast and Dublin. Every evening, my mother asked me to come up and talk to them. She had difficulty attuning to their defences, their lack of responses, and the way they kept themselves at arm's length, especially when she started talking about the past. They behaved like a couple dreading the moment their imposture might come to light. Even the most mundane of conversations had to be avoided, it seemed, in case it set in motion the truth. My mother, who was so kind and considerate, found it hard to be with people who did not meet her gaze, who didn't follow her topics of conversation, who radiated boredom and unease. She took the lack of conversation as a sign that they were unsettled or unhappy and was seized constantly by the need to do something to entertain them. Her predicament was painful for me to watch, but still I kept scurrying up to her dining room every evening, the twilight thickening over the table of family memorabilia. The tea and coffee after dinner sometimes yielded to whiskey, and my mother kept hoping for some memories to emerge amid the awkward conversations.

After each meal, Gregory walked into the garden, lit a fresh cigar and stared at it for a long time as though it were a mysterious clue, while my mother stood at her table of memorabilia, rearranging all the documents and items from her father's life, as if searching for something that had strayed and disappeared without a trace. I could sense the fear of failure in her, the worry that she wasn't getting what she wanted from her guests, that the picture of Patrick Daly had moved a distance away and his story would always be scattered and lost. She knew that something did not quite fit with Gregory's story. She kept moving the details around in the hope that she might find the correct alignment, and now the apprehension was beginning to take hold that her guests might be complete strangers after all, uncovered by accident through the internet and its tangled web of people and events.

A mood of anticipation grew and filled the house. We were waiting for Gregory to find a clue and reveal something new, something that might relate to my mother's granduncle. It was important not to miss the moment. However, days passed, and nothing happened. I sat with them, drinking tea and engaging in small chat, asking questions and watching the expression on Gregory's face, waiting for some sort of change, a story or reminiscence to emerge, a riveting anecdote that he'd heard about his grandfather or father, but we got nothing.

Gregory's reticence allowed for different interpretations. My own pessimistic interpretation, which matched my father's, was that he was play-acting the role of a long-lost relative. When he loosened up after a few whiskies, Gregory spoke like a stereotypical Irish American relative, one with fixed political beliefs drenched in the mythology of Trump's America. He seemed to understand that my mother would like it if he said the expected things. I saw how playing the part of a long-lost relative was easy. He didn't have to work on it at all. The role was made up for him by my mother. He had all the emails from my sister and the story of Patrick Daly's life spread out before him to draw upon.

But who was I to feel superior to him? Wasn't I playing a role for my mother, too, the part of her dutiful son? Were my motives for helping her entertain the couple really that honest and pure? What questions did I hide in my heart? I still hadn't told my mother that I was writing a book about her grandfather and the hijacking. I had to set out the limits of what might be told and what might not. I had to work it out myself. If other people knew what I was doing, then it might become impossible to write the story. I had to set my own limits. They had to come from inside me, and not my mother.

In the evening before their trip along the Atlantic coast, we heard Gregory on the phone in the hall, his voice becoming uncharacteristically high and uncertain. He rattled the receiver back onto the set and made further calls. Afterwards, he and Sarah had a whispered conversation outside the sitting room. When they came in to join us, they behaved as if they had received terrible news from home. Gregory came straight out with it and told my mother their bankcards had been declined. His neck stretched and his complexion deepened. They had no money left. Their flight home wasn't for another six days, and they couldn't afford to make their tour of Ireland. For several moments, they stared at my mother in dreadful silence, Gregory's face darkening.

"Don't worry," said my mother. "You can stay here, and we'll lend you money. Get a good night's sleep and everything will seem better in the morning."

"But we don't want to trouble you anymore," said Gregory.

"No trouble at all."

They allowed her to lead them to their bedroom. Gregory turned at the door. "We'll see you in the morning, then."

"Of course. Breakfast at the usual time." She gave them a reassuring smile. "Good night and sleep well."

In the following days, my mother invited them out on day trips, but they declined her offers. Each day that passed, Gregory grew more morose, and Sarah more anxious, as they counted down the days to their flight. My mother leant them money so they could buy souvenirs for their family back in New Orleans. She even offered to put them up in a hotel in Dublin, but they refused.

I kept getting the call to join them for dinner in the evenings, and my mother would thank me afterwards for trying to strike up conversation. Their financial misfortune appeared to have sealed their mouths. Gregory's eyes fixed on the window and its view of the garden as he ate, while Sarah kept staring at her plate. The vague uneasiness they had transmitted from the start of their visit, I now interpreted as embarrassment or shame.

As I slipped away one evening, my mother grabbed me. "You know, they're beginning to feel like family," she said with a happy glint in her eyes.

A routine set in. The couple moved from room to room, reading the newspapers, watching the television, eating the food my mother laid out for them. Tactfully, she asked no more questions. Gregory and Sarah quickly ran out of conversation, even between themselves, and seemed to be barely on speaking terms with each other. They lived as guests in the centre of the house, but somehow, they managed to absent themselves completely from what my mother or father were doing in the everyday life of the household. Not in the way that Patrick Daly or my grandfather were absent, not like dead people, but more like people who had never existed in the first place.

Who were they? Who they thought they were or who my mother wanted them to be? It was impossible to tell. They seemed lost. Perhaps the past was nothing and they were impostors taking advantage of my mother's hospitality. My mother had her personal vision of who they were, and she stuck with it, even though they outstayed their welcome and borrowed money from her. I tried to warn her that they might be taking advantage of her but deep down I admired the tenacity of her hospitality. In the final days, it struck me that they resembled a pair of harmless resident ghosts, descendants of an adopted orphan, who had travelled all the way to my parent's house to be adopted once again. I told my mother as much, and she laughed. I jokingly warned her she would never be able to make her guests leave, and that she was stuck with them and their living arrangements whether she liked it or not.

In a way, I envied Gregory and Sarah. Their story was not part of my mother's story. They didn't belong to Diseart and that meant they could travel more lightly through the world than I could. Their reliance on my mother's hospitality was a sign of their freedom rather than financial or emotional dependence.

At the end of the fortnight, their leave-taking resembled the closing scene of a play. Shortly after dawn, they emerged from their rooms and stood solemnly in the hall, like actors taking their final bows. I shook hands with them, and we said cheerio, knowing we would probably never meet again.

Gregory stood at the door with his suitcases. He glanced at my dad and me, and then at my mother. He bowed his head as if carefully considering his parting words.

"I'd like to ask you a question before I go, Alice," he said. "That table of memories you've gathered together, do you intend to finish it some day?"

My mother stared at him blankly.

"What I mean is… do you intend to tell the whole story or just limit it to what you want people to know?"

The atmosphere of the house changed. Gregory's heavy presence filled the hall. My mother grimaced slightly. The leave-taking was not going as smoothly as she had planned, and Gregory's question clearly disagreed with her. Suddenly I saw him as one of those popular fictional detectives, shrewd and silent, their silence leading the investigation without anyone noticing.

When she did not reply, Gregory said, "From what you've told me, the table doesn't tell the most important story about Patrick Daly and your father. I think it's time you put that final piece on display."

More silence from my mother. He looked at her and she stared back at him, waiting for him to leave.

"I hope you do some day, Alice. The descendants have a right to know." He stood at the door. For a moment, I thought he was going to wag a disapproving finger at her. Detective Gregory Daley of the New Orleans P.D. was back on duty. My mother's cheeks were blazing, but she said nothing. She didn't even make a gesture. What exactly had she told him? And who were the descendants he was talking about?

"They need to know the truth," he said.

"You're very welcome to come back anytime you want, Gregory," my mother replied in a firm voice. "There'll always be an open door for you in Diseart."

He stroked his chin as if considering the pros and cons of the invitation, and then smiled. "Thank you, Alice. You've been such a wonderful host."

My mother stood at the door and watched my father help them pack their suitcases into the car. She stood for a while, staring into the distance, her grey hair looking ghostly white in the early morning sunlight. The car drove down the road and disappeared around the corner. She closed the front door and walked through the hall without glancing at us.

"Anything to tell us?" I asked her.

"Nothing you don't already know."

"What was Gregory talking about?"

"Just a story I told him."

"What story?"

She pursed her lips.

"You've talked to him about Donaghy," I said. "You must have mentioned something about his murder, some clue, and he's figured it out. Both of you know more than you're telling."

"It was just something I heard through a crack in the door. When I was a child. I can't be sure of it all."

Sensing her weakness, I pressed further. "Was your father in on it? Did he know something about the plan the Hibernians were hatching? That Donaghy was going to be killed?"

Were she and I descendants of a murderer, or an accomplice to murder? And, if so, how would I fit that into my book? The morning sunlight blazed through the kitchen, filling her face with shadows. I peered for a glimpse of her reassuring gaze, but something was weighing heavily on her.

I said, "Patrick's plan to take your father to America must be connected to Donaghy."

"What makes you think that?"

"Surely, it's obvious. To get him away from trouble. Your father was needed on the farm. He was doing a man's work every day. And Patrick must have had a good reason to adopt him when he had already adopted another boy."

She placed her hand on my shoulder and, at once, I grew passive. It was the gesture that always silenced me. In that moment, I sensed that if there was something else to know about Donaghy's murder and my mother hadn't told me, then it would be better not to know. It was time to stop pestering her with questions that might debase the family name, and return to the role of considerate son, who respected and loved his mother and grandfather without conditions.

At times like these, the relationship between my mother and I was the same it had been when I was a teenager. There were so many family stories I didn't know my way around, and nothing that had happened since - the birth of my own children, my career as a journalist and my nine novels - had changed that dynamic. I was the dutiful son, too respectful to really probe into the past or bring up something that might hurt my mother.

And writing all this down was an experiment that would fail because I would never get close to what I really wanted to say about my mother and her father, to write about them in simple terms, about their everyday lives, their love for their families and their deeply rooted sense of place, rather than anything as scandalous and mysterious as an unsolved murder. The truth lay elsewhere, away from my grandfather's arrest and the IRA hijacking, somewhere as yet undiscovered. But the image of my grandfather's bloody handkerchief and the IRA bullet were imprinted in my brain, images that I kept staring at when I couldn't sleep, convinced they were connected and that any attempt to understand why the IRA held my family hostage depended upon that moment when my exhausted grandfather met the police officers waiting at the last bend in the lane.

My mother went into the kitchen and put on the kettle. She assembled some cups with a clatter and returned with a pot of tea. "They wanted my father out of the way," she said.

"Who?"

"The people who murdered Donaghy."

"Why would they want to do that?"

If this was the case, heaven only knew how my

grandfather and his mother took the news of Patrick's death. It must have been hard for them, whatever the reason for his boarding the train.

"That's what I'm still trying to find out," she said.

I looked over at the door to the sitting room and the table of memorabilia within. I could see the picture of Patrick Daly hanging on the wall, taken for the passport that was meant to bring him back to Ireland to rescue his nephew from an unknown threat. The same photo that had helped my mother track him down all these years later. I thought of the nameless railway lines of America, the disappearing trails of lost relatives and the secrets their families had hidden in the bottom of wells, amid the whitethorn hedges, under the dead leaves, and behind the closed doors and dusty attics of an impoverished Irish parish, more secrets than they would ever encounter in their new lives in a new continent. I tried to imagine my grandfather as a young boy, waiting to travel to the U.S., but all I could picture was a circle of neighbours, thin and shadowy, members of the Ancient Order of Hibernians, standing around a boy with a bloody handkerchief.

My mother was busy adding more relatives to her family tree, more witnesses with their shadowy histories, bringing back the story bit by bit of a disarrayed family, poverty-stricken and vulnerable, scuttling between Ireland, Scotland and America. The table of research was growing heavier by the day, and I thought wouldn't it be more merciful to let all the dead Dalys carry their piece of the family story into their graves until there was nothing left to burden the lives of their descendants.

But I was a writer without a story, like a hermit crab in between shells, and I would keep scampering up to my mother's house, greedy for mysteries.

Anthony J. Quinn

1982

Early in the evening, Murphy called with some ice-lollies for the children. The lollies had melted slightly in the heat of his car. Standing at the back door, he took out a handkerchief and carefully wiped his sticky fingers. Then he lit a cigarette and concentrated on smoking. Dermot watched him from the doorstep, recognising the familiar habit of a detective about to say something important.

All week, Murphy had been phoning him, coming up with new assurances to encourage him to help the police investigation. The detective explained that all he was looking for was corroboration of some facts. None of Dermot's evidence was crucial to the prosecution, but it would help tie up some loose ends.

"Forgive me for telling you this," said Murphy after a long pause. "On the morning the IRA gang killed Ivan White, a work colleague of his was driving past the scene. He saw the IRA men shoot Ivan at point blank range and then climb into your car. As they were speeding away, the gunman rolled down the window and shouted, 'Yee-haw'. Ivan was still alive, but bleeding heavily. The colleague shouted for help. There were houses nearby. The people living there would have heard the gunfire, the IRA shouts and the cries for help, but not a single person came to their door to see what had happened."

Murphy grew silent and smoked his cigarette. Dermot didn't know what to say. The detective slowly raised the hand holding the cigarette.

"I've been wondering, when your wife first saw the gunmen in the hedge, why didn't she ring the police? She would have had time to place a call."

Dermot hesitated. How did he know what thoughts had run through her mind that morning? However, he was clear and firm in his answer to the detective. He was the one in charge of telling the story, not his wife. "I don't think it occurred to her at all."

"Did she know they were IRA men? Did she think they might want to hijack your car?" A curl of smoke rose from the cigarette dangling in Murphy's fingers.

"It happened so suddenly." Dermot's right hand trembled slightly.

Murphy noticed the shake and changed the subject. In a gentler voice, he said, "It must be hard for the children with all the intimidation."

"Children are resilient," replied Dermot. "If it doesn't affect them directly, they can ignore almost anything. The rest we try to explain later."

"What did you think about when you saw the news that morning, the pictures of your car, the forensic officers and all that?"

Dermot shrugged his shoulders. "I thought about my car, the forensic officers…"

"But how did it affect you? Or were you able to ignore that?" There was a slight bitterness to Murphy's voice.

Dermot looked at him coldly. "The answers you're looking for are out there," he said, pointing to the landscape of irregular fields leading up to the mountain behind the house.

The detective half-turned. "I think I know what you're saying." He put the cigarette to his lips, inhaled and blew out a quick, tense puff. The fading light gave a blue tone to his hollow cheeks and increased the shadowy circles under his eyes. "This bloody country is full of secrets. We think we know our neighbours and can trust them, but every day, we know them less and less."

Dermot thought of what the detective had said and looked at the twilight fields. For weeks, he hadn't slept properly. Even though it was late April, there was a sharp bite of winter in the air. Shadows contended with the fading daylight, the thorn bushes thronging the borders of fields and filling the little glens.

The detective continued in the same tone. "You might think you know your neighbours, but secrets still remain between you." He was silent for a moment. "And even in families there are secrets. Between parents and children. Even husbands and wives. Alice probably knows things about her neighbours but keeps them hidden from you."

The detective's voice grew hushed. "You've probably noticed a slight change in her when the names of certain neighbours come up in conversation. A difference in her behaviour when you meet them on the road or at Mass."

The wind picked up as the two men stood perfectly still. Dermot considered what Murphy had said. It was true. Alice had been more withdrawn since the hijacking, more absorbed in the secrets of the parish. He stared at the trees and bushes bordering the garden, which seemed to draw closer in the darkness, crowded and watching. In Dermot's tired imagination, the rising wind sounded like the waves of a vengeful sea, and the knobbly blackthorn branches rattled like oars. He could even hear, faintly, the shouting of his night-time visitors. On evenings like these, the thorn trees seemed to pour the shapes of masked men and he kept seeing slashes in the shadows where their eyes flashed at him.

Murphy gave a slight grimace, as though he could sense the images running through Dermot's head.

After the detective returned to his car and drove away, Dermot walked through the back garden to calm his thoughts. Murphy suspected that Alice knew things about the IRA men that he did not, secrets that drew her closer to the other parishioners and away from him. A light switched on in the kitchen. He turned around. His wife stood at the sink, her head slightly bowed. There was a grim expression on her face, and she seemed anchored to the spot, washing the evening dishes. He wondered if the detective's supposition was correct. What intrigues and plots had she inherited? Was she thinking about the gunmen and their families? Unlike her, he did not feel anchored out here in the garden amid the wind-tossed trees, and the days ahead, leading up to the court-case, did not feel anchored, either. He wallowed in the darkness, watching her scrub the pots and pans, undeterred, rooted in their home and family life. He drew closer to the window, unnoticed by her. Even if she were to look up and stare directly into the middle of the garden, she still would not be able to see him. He'd had several conversations with her about the gunmen and their possible identities, but none of them had been enlightening. He had asked her questions about their Republican neighbours, but her answers had been limited, exasperatingly vague, as though she had been talking to a child or a stranger. He felt side-lined, the shadowy figure of a husband, who would always be an outsider no matter how many years he had lived in this parish configured by secrets and family ties. And his wife was changing before his eyes, plunged into the past and the obscure relationships with their neighbours that had been kept hidden from him.

Eventually, he opened the back door, and stepped into the kitchen. The bottoms of his trousers were sodden with the wet grass. He pulled out a seat down and sat down. She raised her hand and placed it on his shoulder.

"At last," she said. "What were you doing standing in the middle of the garden? I've been waiting all this time for you to come in."

2019

Like shadows gliding silently across a darkened sea, the microfiched pages of the Tyrone Chronicle newspaper swept before my eyes. I was sitting on the second floor of the local library scanning through the archived reports from 1982. The names of vanished advertising brands and nightclubs flashed past in black and white, the microfiche reader humming through the scrolls with surprising force, but I was searching for something more macabre - the black bordered headlines that signalled reports about murder. Each time I froze the images, I felt a tremor of foreboding.

According to the front pages of the Chronicle, the year began in horror and blood. A young Protestant man died from his injuries after the IRA detonated a bomb in a Cookstown bar during a New Year's party. The revenge attack took place a week later in Coagh. A fake checkpoint manned by loyalists shot dead two young Catholic men returning from a football match. I followed the murderous cycle through February and March, each murder rooted in the savagery that preceded it, names and dates flickering by without registering or offering me any clues, and then in April, I found several reports of Ivan White's murder and a brief mention of the hijacking. I had never sought out the news stories of that morning, and I felt an instinctive recoil. My mind filled with images of twisting lanes and burnt-out cars, checkpoints in the dark, the blood-spattered porches of isolated farms and hooded men roaming the darkness. A bloody darkness welled up behind the newsprint, and I was confronted by a feeling of helplessness. How was I to dissect the events of such a brutal year?

I flicked through the weekly editions, scanning forward into May and June. I sifted through the news pages and sighed. From my post near the library window, I could hear the town church bells marking out the quarters of the hour. I waded through more reports of bombings and shootings, funerals and court cases, photographs of dead soldiers, police officers, and civilians. The Protestant paramilitaries would kill some Catholics, and then the IRA would kill some soldiers or police officers; the familiar pattern repeating itself. I stared blankly through the library window, coldness gripping my stomach. I didn't believe in pure evil or that brutality was written into the genes of my neighbours. I wanted to believe that the circumstances, the environment had been evil during that time in the 1980s, and not the people of Tyrone. But 1982 had been a dark year.

I scanned forward into July and then I found a report about a SAS ambush near Ballygawley. Three young IRA men from the parish of Diseart had been killed after fruitlessly launching a mortar bomb attack on a heavily fortified army base. I stared at the police mug shots of the dead men, faces tipped back in defiance and contempt, barely out of adolescence, sharp-featured, unwrinkled by the signs of age. Three young men bound together by a code of violence. I recognised their names and some of their facial features. My parents had mentioned them before as prime suspects in the hijacking. At last, I had their faces and personal details. I could weave stories about them, trace their family connections to neighbours and friends in the parish. Each had a history of prior convictions, membership of the IRA, possession of weapons, and had been on the run since the hijacking of our car. They'd changed their hairstyles, let their moustaches and sideburns grow out. They'd become lean and haggard, hiding in outhouses, forests and pokey attics. I checked what had been written about them on the internet. Apart from their violent deaths, there was little evidence they had occupied the planet for any length of time.

The SAS ambush marked the end of the IRA gang's campaign, and there was a reduction in the number of bombing or shooting incidents in the weeks that followed. However, there was no mention in any of the reports of a fourth member of the gang. The eyes and beards of the men in the mugshots didn't seem to resemble the IRA man who had given me the bullet. What had happened to him? Had he managed to escape or was his disappearance part of something sinister? Had he been somehow blackmailed by the security forces into betraying his comrades? And if so, had the IRA interrogated him? If they had suspected he was an informer, they would have shot him within a couple of days of the ambush. But there were no reports in the weeks that followed of a dead IRA informer found with a bullet in his head.

I was so absorbed that at first, I didn't hear my mobile phone ringing. It was Frances, my wife. I slipped outside to the stairwell and took the call.

"Someone just called to see you," she said. "A man called Malachy Warde."

"What did he want?"

"He didn't say. I told him you were in the town and would be back this evening."

A figure emerged from the floor above and glanced down the stairwell at me. It was a man with piercing green eyes. I almost dropped the phone in surprise. The man's eyes were very green, but not as green as Warde's.

Warde had probably come to my house to gloat. The day previously, the front page of the Irish News had been plastered with the story of the missing gun he'd told me about on the night of the wake, and the police attempts to cover up its discovery. I'd played a small role in bringing the story to light. After the night of the wake, I'd sent a request off to the police press office, asking questions about the gun. Unsurprisingly, they hadn't replied, and so I'd passed the details on to a journalist at the Irish News, someone who I knew would pursue the story with more tenacity and brio.

"What's wrong?" asked Frances.

"Nothing." Briefly, I explained Warde's history to her, the story he'd asked me to research and the newspaper revelations. Then I told her about the hijacking reports I'd found and how I was convinced the IRA man who'd given me the bullet had escaped the SAS ambush that killed his comrades. What if he'd betrayed his comrades and sent them to their deaths? I wondered. What if he was some sort of informer?

There was a lengthy pause from her. "I think it's strange," she said. "You have a creepy IRA man calling to our door asking you to investigate a missing gun and you're getting excited in the library about something that happened nearly forty years ago."

"You're not interested?"

"What about the crime novel you're writing?"

"This is the crime novel I'm writing. And now I've finally worked out what the central mystery will be – the identity of the IRA man who gave me the bullet and what happened to him."

"But that's a true story. Have you thought of the consequences? How will his family react for a start?"

It was my duty to record what had happened and probe the shadows, I said.

"To record, yes, but what you're doing is digging for something sensational. That's what journalists do, not writers. You're not a journalist anymore. And anyway, you can't just write this story and walk away from it. These are your neighbours you're writing about. Think of the consequences."

Consequences. That word again. Did my neighbours or the IRA think of it on the morning of the hijacking? Shouldn't a writer have the courage to tell a difficult story rather than worry about what happened afterwards? I felt a ruthless streak take hold. I had to finish the book and not worry about the consequences.

"I need to track down this missing IRA man. I have to ask him some questions."

"Why do that? What has any of this to do with right now, our family, our life in Diseart? What good will it do anyone?"

Most likely, very little, I thought. But I still wanted to find out the truth.

I went back to the microfiche and printed out the reports of the SAS ambush and the funeral services of the three IRA men. I stared at the images of their faces and thought about what Frances had said. Their faces stared back at me with features ready to fling themselves into rage at what I was doing, daring to write about them all these years later, violating the sacrifice of their death, raising questions about their missing comrade. I examined their sharp cheekbones and tousled hair, the tilt of their noses and the wildness in their eyes. They were handsome young men, Tyrone's finest, devoured by the blind Cronus of the Republican creed, and almost forgotten by history. But where was the fourth member of the gang? Deprived of a name, deprived of a violent death or a long prison sentence, he had vanished in the way a plane suddenly vanishes from a radar.

I left the library and drove home, deep in thought. Apart from my parents and the hijackers, one other person had been there in 1982, a person close to the investigation who might be able to shed some light on the mysterious fourth gunman. A detective who knew my father from childhood, who used to pull up to the house in a nondescript car at the oddest of hours. I could still recall his name, Brian Murphy. The image of him talking to my father about their school days in the kitchen spoke to me from a distant and unreachable past. Murphy had been an intriguing figure, well-dressed, but a little rough looking, the embodiment of a dogged kind of detective confidence. He had entered our family life like a long-lost but slightly disreputable relative, chatting to my father while my mother frowned in the background. I could still picture my father listening to him, his face turned slightly away from the detective, looking out the window or at the floor, but not really looking at anything.

After the court case had collapsed, Murphy never returned to our house, and I couldn't recall my father ever mentioning him again. Was he still alive? I wondered. What secrets might he know? I had to do something. I had to make some sort of breakthrough that would help solve the mystery of the fourth gunman.

During my time as a reporter at the local newspaper, I had been on friendly terms with a Chief Inspector based at Dungannon Police Station, a tall, dignified man called Tom Wilson, who had sported an impressively thick black moustache. After one of the Monday mornings press briefings, he mentioned that he'd enjoyed reading my debut novel. I'd rushed to reassure him that the Chief

Inspector called Tom Donaldson in the book hadn't been based on him at all, but I had borrowed his moustache and his Christian name. Wilson later shaved his moustache and retired, but I still had his mobile number somewhere.

Wilson was a jovial and friendly on the phone as he'd been at the weekly press briefings. "It's late," he said. "You writers work nights, too."

After I'd explained the story I was working on, he asked, "How can I help?"

"There's a detective I need to find. A man called Brian Murphy. He was based in the Dungannon area in the 1980s."

Wilson grew guarded. He had known Brian Murphy; the last he'd heard, Murphy had retired and was living in Belfast. He promised to ask around and get me a contact number.

Two days later, I got a text from Wilson with a mobile number and a message that said good luck. I dialled the number but there was no answer. I tried several times without success. Eventually, I left Murphy a recorded message introducing myself in as friendly a voice as possible. I didn't want to unnerve him. I could only guess at how unsettling it might be for a retired detective to get a call out of the blue about an unfinished case.

1982

Dermot drained his cup of tea and stared at Detective Murphy, wondering how much of his silences would be reported back to Murphy's superiors. Their conversation had been long and full of awkward pauses, but there was something he wanted to get off his chest, and Murphy seemed in no hurry to leave.

"Every night I can't stop thinking about the hijackers," said Dermot.

Murphy rubbed his jaw and thought for a moment. "You don't think about Ivan White every night?"

"No."

But he did think about the dead policeman often, lying in a pool of his blood while the IRA men shouted yeehaw from the family car, and each time with a troubled conscience. "Should I be thinking about him every night?"

Murphy seemed about to say something that Dermot was sure he would not like to hear, but the detective let it go.

"No, why should you?" said Murphy looking away. "I'm sure Protestants don't think about their murdered Catholic neighbours every night."

Dermot wanted to say something more, that the guilt he felt about the dead policeman had grown daily and would always be a part of who he was, and that only an insane person would feel blameless or walk away without any scars from such an ordeal. But the truth of the matter was he had not done anything wrong. He hadn't driven the car or pulled the trigger. He had hurt no one.

In a neutral tone of voice, Dermot said, "I've been mulling over something you told me about the court case."

"I've said a lot of things about the court case."

"You told me it would clear my name."

"Did I say that?"

"Yes, you did."

"Well, what I meant was the court case would tell the truth and clear away the false suspicions." Murphy paused. "Isn't that what our justice system is supposed to do?"

"I don't need the justice system to clear my name. I'm not a murderer or a criminal."

"I can see you're annoyed, Dermot."

"The IRA gave my eldest son a bullet. They said they would use it to shoot me if I rang the police before one o'clock. They took our car and left us without transport."

Murphy nodded.

"I can't fight the IRA on my own."

"You're right. Enough people have died at their hands already."

There was a slight surliness about Murphy. Perhaps he was tired after working a long shift. It occurred to Dermot that the detective might have been irritated by his complaint about having no car. Or maybe Murphy was having doubts about where Dermot's allegiances lay, with the side of law and order or his Republican neighbours.

Dermot was curious about Murphy's own family. After all, it must be hard working as a Catholic detective in the Royal Ulster Constabulary and keeping one's family safe.

"I hardly ever see them," said Murphy in a resentful tone when Dermot brought up the subject. "So, don't ask me about them again." His eyes were shadowed. "Lots of policemen have to live with threats, not just the Catholic ones."

I'm sure they did, thought Dermot. He decided not to mention Murphy's family again, but it seemed strange the detective did not want talk about them. For a moment, Dermot imagined that the detective might not be who he said he was, that he only bore a passing resemblance to the Brian Murphy who had been his childhood pal. Perhaps the detective was the old Brian Murphy but with a new set of allegiances and values, the same physical person but with a different code, a different way of looking at history, a different personality swapped at the start of the Troubles. Dermot poured some more tea and sipped from his cup. The conversations with Murphy tended to leave his throat dry.

The detective refused Dermot's offer of more tea and hitched himself forward in his chair. "Actually, there's something I've been meaning to bring up, Dermot. It concerns a record in a file one of my colleagues dug up." He lowered his voice. "It's to do with a Civil Rights march in Dungannon in 1970. You were arrested on a charge of breaking the peace."

Dermot hadn't expected this to come up. He did not deny to Murphy that he had taken part in the Civil Rights march or that he had been briefly arrested and detained, but he did his best to distort the events of the day. He had been a youth, he explained, an innocent bystander caught up in what had begun as an amusing adventure but had quickly deteriorated into a riot after the police fired bullets.

"You were just a bystander?"

"Yes."

"You didn't throw stones at the police?"

"No." Dermot tried to see the detective's eyes, but Murphy had bowed his head. "Why bring this up? What has it to do with the hijacking?"

Murphy glanced up at him sharply, a look of suspicion forming in his eyes. It was as if by questioning the detective's approach, Dermot had declared his hostility to Murphy and the police investigation. At once, the detective's tone changed.

"You might think it's none of our business, but this is a murder investigation. Some of my colleagues have raised questions."

"What sort of questions?"

"They wonder if you ever were an I...R...A... man."

The way Murphy elongated the letters sent a shiver down Dermot's spine. "I've never been a member of the IRA or any paramilitary organisation."

Dermot had no idea how much Murphy knew about his involvement with the Civil Rights Movement. He might know a lot more than he claimed. In all likelihood, he had recounted only a little of what he did know, but there was one thing Dermot was now sure of: the purpose of the detective's visits was less to probe the guilt of his neighbours than the innocence of Dermot and his wife. The detective was a bloodhound and now that he had got a scent, he would not give up the chase.

Murphy placed his cup of tea on the table. "Tell me," he said. "What happened when the IRA hijackers walked into your house? What exactly did they say and do?"

"I've told you that a dozen times."

"Just one more time. You probably know it off by heart by now."

"All right." He told Murphy he had been woken by the sound of heavy footsteps in the hall. He had got up but there was no sign of his wife and children. He walked into the hall and found the IRA gang standing together with balaclavas and guns. He and Alice never used to lock the front door, but things had definitely changed since. "The gunmen made their announcement and demanded the keys to our car. It was about half seven. Then they herded us into the living room at gunpoint."

"Was that all?"

"Yes."

The detective hesitated for a few seconds. "Is there anything else you can add? Something that might be helpful?"

"No. Not a thing."

"What about the conversation the gang leader had with your wife? When he took her into a room and closed the door. I'm talking about the one with the ginger beard."

Dermot reeled a little from Murphy's knowledge of that conversation. Neither he nor his wife had ever mentioned it before.

"Who told you about that?" he asked.

"Is there a problem? Is what I said inaccurate?"

"No. It's just that I'm surprised you know about it." Dermot said that Alice had never brought it up in the interviews, and he hadn't either, not wanting to draw unnecessary police attention to her.

"I'm a thorough detective," said Murphy. "I don't rest until I know everything I need to know." He gave a faint smile. "You'd be amazed at the intelligence resources the police have at their disposal."

Dermot considered the possibility that the police had bugged their home. His cheeks began to glow. To hide his annoyance and signal the end of their conversation, he leaned forward to take away Murphy's empty cup, but the detective gestured for him to sit back in his chair.

"You haven't answered my question."

"What question?"

"Is there anything else you can remember about that morning?"

"You're right. One of the IRA men did take Alice into a room and talked to her. He warned her not to speak to the police. He said my life was in danger. That's all there was to it."

"Neither of you mentioned it earlier. I'm curious to know why."

"We didn't think it was important. And to tell you the truth, I'd rather you keep my wife out of this investigation. She's the mother of five young children."

"Well, thank you, again, Dermot." The detective glanced at his watch. "And thanks for the tea. I don't need to ask Alice anything else, at least for now."

2019

When I opened the front door to Malachy Warde, he immediately narrowed the distance between us. "I've come to talk to you about the gun story," he said with such intensity that I could do nothing but step aside and usher him into the house.

I glanced uneasily through the trees at my parent's house and closed the door. For years, my father had been nipping in the bud any attempts made by our Republican neighbours at closer ties. Fund-raisers for ex-prisoners, Sinn Fein councillors seeking election and even the ticket sellers for Irish Language organisations, he dispatched with surly inhospitality. I had followed his example, discouraging such callers with a simple but courteous dismissal. Fortunately, my parent's house was completely hidden by the spring foliage. If my father knew that Warde was standing on my doorstep, he'd have taken his shotgun from the trunk under his bed and loaded it with buckshot.

Warde wore a wide grin as he slunk into the living room. "We have them on the run, now. Did you read in the Irish News what their excuse was? About how detectives thought the gun was an antique from World War One and ignored it?"

I nodded.

"They've got a fine turn of phrase, haven't they?" he said. "I couldn't stop grinning when I read it."

I bet you couldn't, I thought.

"Trying to cover up this weapon was the stupidest thing they could have done. The weekend newspapers are going to make a meal out of it. There's more revelations to come in the Sunday World." He stared at me. "Would you like to hear another story, one that's right up your street?"

"What sort of story?"

He glanced through the door at two of my daughters, who were standing in the hall, staring at him. "Maybe you'd better close that door," he said.

After I'd asked the girls to play in the kitchen, he told me the story of a young man who had disappeared while walking home from a local dance hall at the start of the Troubles. Eyewitnesses had seen him being picked up by a car driven by two men. A few days later, his body was found at a scenic spot popular with lovers. Warde said the police had arrested and questioned the wrong men, later releasing them without charge. However, the finger of blame had always marked them, blighting their young lives. Years later, after the investigation collapsed, the victim's father had contacted Warde in desperation, hoping that he might hold some sway over the community and break the wall of silence. Warde had asked questions and was convinced the police investigation had been a cover-up, designed to hide the identity of one of the guilty parties, a relative of a serving police officer. He went over the same points several times, the carelessness of the police investigation, the lack of cooperation from the eyewitnesses and the wall of silence in the community.

When he had finished, he hunched forward. "What do you think? Isn't that a tale that deserves to be told?"

I told him he was right, but as I spoke, another story was revolving in my mind, one much closer to home. I had waited for him to make the first move, to tell his tale, and now it was my turn.

"I'm working on a similar type of story myself," I said.

He raised an eyebrow. "About what?"

I was no longer a floundering, ignorant reporter

following his lead, and what I was about to ask him represented a dangerous transgression. But if my story was about anything, it was about overcoming the fear of transgression. I was no longer afraid of him. That was the truth of the matter. Besides, he owed me a favour and I was too confident to stop. And when would I get a chance to quiz him again? He was clearly in good form, and I felt invulnerable sitting in my own living room. I told myself mothing was random in the parish of Diseart. Everything was connected. You cannot choose a story. Rather, a story chooses you and you must take what it gives. Warde had been sent to my door that evening to bring me to a new understanding of the hijacking. This was my turn, my story, my questions.

"The story is about a couple of things," I said. "Including the IRA hijacking of our car in 1982."

Warde said nothing, but his eyes bulged, and the grin disappeared from his face.

"One thing puzzles me," I said. "Everyone talks about the three men in that IRA gang." I listed their names. "But there were four men in our house that morning, not three. No one ever talks about the fourth gunman."

He moved as if he were about to rise from his chair and leave, but he didn't. He wavered, disconcerted slightly. He sat still without taking his eyes off me.

"That's a completely different kind of story," he said eventually. There was a new edge to his voice. His face was heavy, solemn with shadows. I had seen the same resolute expression on my mother's face when I asked her questions about the hijacking.

"What do you want to know?"

"The fourth gunman's name."

"Why do you want to know?"

"Because I want to set the record straight."

This time the silence seemed to last forever. From the kitchen, I could hear dishes and conversation. Warde scrutinised me with a slight tilt of his head.

"There's not much of a story to it," he said eventually. "But you're right, no one ever talks about the fourth man, or mentions his name these days. The entire parish has stopped thinking about him."

I could see the spark of interest in his eyes. However, he wasn't interested in the nameless IRA man. He was more interested in the story I was writing and what I was going to do with it.

"This story of yours, is it for a newspaper?"

"No. I'm thinking of weaving it into a work of fiction."

He sank back into his seat and seemed to relax. He was wise enough to know that the gulf between a true story and a work of fiction could be enormous, as wide as an ocean. Still, he approached my question cautiously, step by step.

"Who do *you* think it was?" he asked.

There were several names in my head, but I wasn't going to fall into his trap. I told him I hadn't a clue who it was.

"Explain to me what happens in this fictional story of yours."

"I can't." I couldn't even explain it to myself. The thought crossed my mind that he might be buying time to prepare an answer.

"It doesn't sound like you're getting very far with it."

For several moments, neither of us spoke. His eyes were locked on mine. Neither of us showed any inclination to break the silence, but when I opened my mouth to ask the question again, he spoke first.

"Did your mother ever tell you anything about the hijacking?"

For the first time, I felt the touch of a dangerous probe.

"We've talked about it and the intimidation afterwards. There was a court case, but it collapsed."

"Did she give you any names?"

"No. No names."

"What about your neighbours? Have you talked to them?"

"I'm not interested in gossip. I want the truth."

"Well, it's no big secret," he said off-handedly. "His name was Dominic Hughes. No one in the parish talked about him because no one wanted to implicate an active volunteer. We're talking about a family man with young children. They were a close outfit, the four of them. They acted as back-up and cover for each other and stuck together through thick and thin."

"If they were so close, why wasn't he with them on the night of the SAS ambush?"

He looked at me steadily and then grunted. "Dominic had been stood down a few weeks before the ambush. He'd been involved in a punch-up outside a pub with some local hoods. He was in the process of getting a severe kicking when he pulled out a gun, stuck it in the face of one of the yobbos and told them all he was in the IRA. The hoods scarpered but Dominic's fate was sealed. The army council thought he was too big a security risk and removed him from active duties."

"Sounds like he got a lucky break," I said.

Warde flashed a lifeless smile. "You might say that. Or you might say he was denied an honourable death. A few years later he was killed in a car-crash. Drink-driving."

It wasn't the story I wanted to hear, but at least I now had a name.

"Where's he buried?"

"Cloghgar Chapel." He leaned forward with his unstable eyes. "Does that satisfy your curiosity?"

1982

"Is everything all right, Dermot?" said Alice as they sat down at the kitchen table before bedtime.

He looked up and gave her an uneasy smile. "I was just thinking about something."

"Anything important?"

He thought now might be a good time to ask her what had happened when the IRA leader took her into the room on her own. He hesitated. Perhaps it would be better not to trouble her or involve her any further with the investigation.

"Has Murphy brought up something new?" she asked.

"Yes and no."

She glanced at him. "Meaning you don't want to tell me."

He took a gulp of tea. "No, not at all."

Alice took her cup of tea in both hands and placed it against her cheek, just below her ear. She studied Dermot closely. The phone rang in the hall and she got up and answered it. There was a moment of silence before she carefully replaced the receiver.

"Who was it?"

"Don't ask," she said and slumped in her chair. She seemed more tired than he was. All these years, the two of them had been pulling in tandem at the same load, raising their five children and creating a home in Diseart, but now it was as if she was labouring under a new burden. Her face was thinner than ever, and her mouth wore that distinctive downturned expression she had inherited from her father, her lips pursed, as if holding back some crucial point.

"Murphy seems to know a lot about the hijacking," said Dermot. "More than we told him. He knows one of them had a ginger beard and took you into the kitchen for a talk. I don't know where he got that information from."

Alice rose and put the kettle on. She waited for it to boil.

"Sometimes, I feel he's testing me," said Dermot. He's making up details that are false just to see if I'm tempted to lie. And then he throws in something true that we never told him."

"You've been going over this in your head for too long."

"But don't you see? He's a detective. He shouldn't be mixing lies with the truth. If confuses people."

The phone rang, and annoyance rose in Dermot's chest. It was as if the caller had given them just enough time to settle back into their conversation before disturbing them again. They stared at each other, tight-lipped. It rang nineteen times before stopping.

"Persistent," said Dermot.

Almost immediately, the phone rang again. Once more, they counted nineteen rings.

"Creatures of habit, too," said Alice.

This time, they found it impossible to resume their conversation. When the phone rang for the fourth time, Dermot marched into the hall and unplugged the phone from the socket.

In his dreams that night, he saw the masked face of an IRA man in the mirror. The gunman was his reflection, he realised. In protecting the gunman's identity, he was protecting himself. That was the secret truth in the night-time taunts. The truth is you are our double, was the IRA's haunting message. In defending your family, you are defending us. So, forget about saving your soul or soothing your conscience. Say nothing to the police, say nothing at all.

2019

After Warde's visit, a bout of writer's block overtook me, and I fumbled over my keyboard for several nights, struggling to write anything further about the missing IRA man. I started and gave up various versions of my grandfather's story, hoping to piece it together with the events of 1982. In search of inspiration, I went for long walks, moping around the parish like a dog that had lost its scent. I walked the familiar route between my parent's farmhouse and the cottage where my mother grew up, now abandoned and used as a cowshed by a neighbouring farmer, the white parish church with its square tower, which my grandfather had helped build, and, along the way, the hidden springs and little glens of holly and hazel.

I explored the small fields of my grandfather's farm, trailing through hummocky grass and peering into thickets of blackthorns. It was a lob-sided landscape, rising quirkily and dipping into little streams and marshy bogs. This part of the parish was known as Fashglashagh, which my Irish teacher had once translated as 'the watery wilderness'. As a boy, I had loved exploring its spongy boundaries and its profusion of springs shimmering in the sunlight.

No doubt something violent and glacial had once passed through Fashglashagh, twisting the symmetry of the landscape. The land was always sinking and rising, and men and women like my grandfather and his mother had contained the land with their spades and ploughs, digging drains, cleaning out ditches, unblocking wells, soothing and curbing the unstable water that lay beneath.

My grandfather's mother spent the coldest months of the year cleaning the brimming ditches of the fields she rented, and I could imagine her silent vigilance as she patrolled the brink between land and water. Generations of her family had done the same, managing this equilibrium between the elements.

I was searching for the credentials of my grandfather's generation, the men and women who had been tenant farmers in this impoverished landscape. They'd grown up in meadows covered in bitter sorrel, water-mint and sloeberries. All their lives, they'd been nourished by this watery wilderness. They'd never known acres of green pasture, fertile fields of grain, or potato drills clear of stones and boggy hollows. They were reared amid springs that shifted and shimmered underfoot, overflowing wells, narrow fields that flooded every winter and were home to strange vapours, rows of mouldy crops, weed-filled ditches that had to be cleared every year, bankrupt farms and rotting cottages, a landscape that penetrated to the marrow of their bones and made them constantly fearful. Watching over them always was the remote but ever so close figure of the landlord, his silent bureaucracy indifferent to the hardship of toiling in such a landscape.

The more I walked and thought of my grandfather's world, the more my understanding of the parish and its landscape expanded. Not that I would ever understand every contour, or penetrate every shadow, but I was moving towards a vision of coherence, one that absorbed my grandfather's lost meadows and caught his inner landscape.

I found new vantage points of the tree-filled hollow I shared with my parent's and my three sisters with their young families, all daughters, and no sons. It struck me that I was always father, son, and brother at the same time in this landscape, and often the father in me was struggling against the son in me. I was trapped in Diseart, surrounded by too much home, but my thoughts were focused elsewhere, in another version of reality. One part of me was sinking deeper into my roots, and the other was struggling to get away, to evoke a freer world in my writing.

Some days, I felt a prisoner in a sanctuary of women: my wife, my mother, my three sisters, my daughters and nieces - an entire social order based on one gender, a whole tribe of females to whom I was bound with love and tenderness and followed every day along the predictable rails of routine. But what of the other man in this colony of women and children? Where was my father, Dermot, and his story in this merry-go-round of families and houses? What about the fellowship of fathers and sons?

My dad, and the world of his thoughts and feelings, was almost invisible to me. He was a back door closing in a house I'd just entered, a silhouette glimpsed through a window or a figure in the rain hurrying to his jeep on another errand for a DIY project or some message for my mother. At 73, he was still fit and able, preoccupied completely by practical tasks, and always seemed to float above the disarray of having three of his children raising families with their spouses on top of his own household. The children of his neighbours had grown up and moved away, families came and went, and marriages broke up, while he strode between houses and women, fixing central heating systems, checking on the wiring and plumbing, tinkering with cars and mowing neglected lawns, or looking after his granddaughters, sitting quietly at a kitchen table and watching them do their homework.

Sometimes, we took shelter together from the rain, in a shed or garage, surrounded by equipment and bric-a-brac, and chatted a little, but our natural silences always took over. We watched the steam of our breaths mingle or listened to the sound of the rain, and then we'd scuttle back to our separate houses, recognising something fugitive in the other, our masculinity somehow vulnerable. Life at home was so predictable, controlled and safe. I had to make myself write every day to feel any hint of danger or trespass. Writing about the past was fraught with danger, but it was also a way of expressing and exerting myself. Every time I turned an empty page, the world opened, and I felt a shiver of excitement.

My grandfather's childhood had been rough and miserable, ravaged by poverty, illness and a violent political climate, but it had also produced him, a man of great contentment and gentle humour. I was my grandfather's heir but also his shadow. By remaining at home, I was prolonging his link to the stingy soil of Diseart. I had stayed behind while all my friends at school had moved to different parts of the globe. And now I was usurping his memory, his boggy fields and bloody handkerchief, using my imagination to make a story out of his past. In writing, I was trespassing.

There was one version of the story, so ordinary and prosaic that it was barely a story. My grandfather had led a clear and simple life, unburdened by guilt or memories of violence. And then there was the version I was trying to write, to which I was attaching scraps of rumour and family folklore, and now these fragmentary reports of a missing IRA man. Was finishing the book more important to me than telling the truth? I could no longer trust my own intentions. When I read back through what I had written, it no longer felt like a true tale, more like one of those stories that are handed down through the generations and slowly ripen into a folk tale.

If I was creating anything truthful out of all these scraps of stories, it was the landscape of Diseart, this hinterland of bubbling springs and secrets. The landscape stretched before me, and I smiled at the thought of it. I should let its stories find me, and trust them, not my own intentions.

1982

While Alice slept motionlessly, Dermot moaned and cursed in his sleep. In the middle of the night, he woke, unable to breathe with the emotional tension, his mind seesawing between the faces of Murphy and those of the IRA hijackers. When a pair of car headlights sliced through the night, lighting up the bedroom ceiling, and the taunts of their persecutors shattered the silence, he opted for a spontaneous solution to their predicament. Rolling out of bed, he crept across the landing to the cupboard where he had locked his shotgun. He wrenched the key around in the lock and the door opened with a clatter. He stood still, waiting for a noise from the bedroom.

After several moments, he lifted the gun, feeling a new and strange sensation of power take hold. He hurried down the stairs, his free hand scrabbling for the banisters to steady his balance. The shouts were more distinct in the hallway, and the lights of the cars shone brightly through the windows. The voices rang in his ears and their lights guided him through the house towards the back door.

He didn't want to surrender to the miserable, claustrophobic life imposed by his IRA neighbours, but nor was he trying to be a hero. The time for being a hero was on the morning of the hijacking when there was still time to stop the gunmen in their tracks. He wished he could march back to that morning with his gun and refuse to hand over the keys of his car. It was the first moments of their ordeal that distressed him the most. The fact that he had allowed the IRA into their home. He could have refused to hand over the keys or phoned the police as soon as the gunmen left, but he hadn't. He didn't belong to the tiny minority of people prepared to sacrifice their lives and the safety of their family. He belonged to the tribe of decent but degraded Catholic men and women, and now, goaded and persecuted by his neighbours, he was ready to throw caution to the wind.

The time to be a miserable puppet was over. The time for passivity was over. All his common sense and reason dissolved into an angry tumult as he opened the door and rushed towards the car headlights, the double-barrelled shotgun thrust before him like a sword.

2019

Cloghgar Chapel was a tidy but rather gloomy little building, barely half the size of the church in Diseart and perched on the side of a windswept mountain. The graveyard was small, too, with neat rows of leaning headstones, and I figured it would not take me too long to find Dominic Hughes' grave. I was still curious about what had happened to the man. I wanted to find his final resting place, say a prayer and ask the questions I had wanted him to answer.

I wandered amid the graves, the decorative stones sparkling in the spring sunshine. I peered and snooped amid the shadows of headstones. I studied the inscriptions. So many of them bore the same surnames - Kelly, Rafferty, O'Hagan, McStay – that there seemed to be something fiercely exclusive about the way the dead had been gathered here on this dark mountainside, as though the graveyard were unwilling to accommodate outsiders. I wormed my way to the Republican burial plot, a prominent site reserved for IRA volunteers, male and female. Hughes was most likely buried here, amid the shiny murals and expensive looking memorial stones.

I read the inscriptions and dedications. The sickly mythology of sacrifice and martyrdom in this part of the graveyard made me uneasy. Even in the tiny parish of Cloghgar, it had consumed so many souls. It suggested that death had been the only instrument these young men had at their disposal to achieve their political goals, and the youthful gunmen who'd hijacked our car, so full of conviction and vehemence, had been half-dead already.

Waging murder was the last link that united them with the world of the living. But what about the IRA men who'd been too alive to die with their comrades? What had happened to them? I wondered. The questions troubled me as I searched for Hughes' grave.

I could find no sign of his name. I looked up and all around. Below the cemetery lay a valley and wave after wave of low black hills, loosely knitted with brilliant yellow gorse. A cold wind picked up and a shower of needling rain fell. I took shelter in the lee of the chapel, wedging myself tight against the rough walls, watching the graveyard grow dimmer.

The rain stopped as soon as it started. The clouds surged away, and the sun came out. I heard a dry cough and someone clearing their throat. I looked around the corner and saw an old man with a long, wooden-handled spade bending down to scrape the weeds from the footpaths. I thought I should sound him out. He was most likely the gravekeeper, and if he didn't know where Hughes grave lay, no one would.

"Morning," I said.

He gave me a polite nod, but there was a shrewd-looking scowl to his face.

"I'm looking for the grave belonging to Dominic Hughes."

Slowly, he straightened his back. He stroked his beard, which was shimmering with raindrops. "He would be one of the Dunfanaghy Hugheses. They lie next to the Kellys from Mullaghfoyle. On the other side of the Red Loughrans."

He waved in the direction of a yew tree, his bony finger tracing out an invisible set of grid lines. However, I had already searched that corner. I gave him a puzzled look.

"Follow the path all the way up to Eddie O'Neill's headstone," he said.

Most of the gravestones there were old and fuzzy-lettered, and probably belonged to the 19th Century. He must have seen the look on my face. He put down his spade with a sigh and ambled in the direction of the yew-tree. I followed him until he stopped and pointed to an untidy looking grave, its headstone carved from some sort of black stone with a gold-lettered inscription. I read what it said and instantly realised I had wasted a journey. The Dominic Hughes buried here had died in 1981. A year before the hijacking. He couldn't have been the fourth member of the IRA gang.

The old man saw my disappointed reaction.

"Not the right grave?" he asked.

"No. Definitely not. The man I'm looking for was alive in 1982."

"A man you're looking for. Not a grave." His face sharpened with curiosity.

"Yes," I replied. "Would there be another Dominic Hughes buried here, one who died in a car accident in the mid-80s?"

"We've only one Dominic Hughes buried here. Would you like to see another grave?"

I shook my head.

1982

Alice woke to an empty bed, lights flashing across the bedroom walls and the sounds of car engines revving outside. She called Dermot's name. When there was no reply, fear rose in her throat. Downstairs, the back door clicked open and slammed shut. She rushed to the window and saw the shape of her husband stumbling outside with a rifle in his outstretched arms. She banged the glass pane and shouted. He turned round, lit up by the car headlights. His vacant eyes stared up at her with the gaze of a man lost in his own nightmare and about to step across a threshold into a wild place, a man with no sense of the terrible danger he was in.

She dashed downstairs, still in her nightgown, and out into the night. She grabbed his pyjama top and with a violent jerk, hauled him back, but he shook her off and stormed forward. She pleaded with him, on the verge of tears; for the first time in her life, she cursed at him. She saw his hard face in the headlights, his eyes glittering. No more signs of weakness or passivity there. He looked furious in his determination to take on their persecutors.

He advanced towards the cars, their engines roaring in response, his silhouette and that of the gun clearly outlined, an obvious target if one of the drivers chose to accelerate forward. She stopped at the edge of the light, not wanting to make herself a target, too. She watched him raise the gun and take aim. She screamed and his face turned towards her, ghostly pale, glaring at her, the same look she'd seen in the eyes of the gunmen on the morning of the hijacking. Recognition rang in her mind like a bell, and she saw what she had been trying to forget, the unmasked faces of the gunmen in the hedgerows, their eyes shining with the hysteria of bloodthirsty men, their deformed silhouettes creeping towards her, now fusing in the intense light of the car headlamps.

The driver of the closest car gave more throttle, as if goading Dermot to shoot. Exhaust fumes and the smell of terror filled her nostrils. Suddenly, more shapes appeared out of the murk of the garden, two shadows, striding towards Dermot. Alice shouted a warning and then froze. There was something familiar about the shadows, the stooped shoulders of the larger one, the confident but careful steps, and the smaller one moving less stiffly, hurrying and guiding the other. She couldn't tell if they were men or women. She could only see their outlines, blending and merging with other silhouettes, the trees and bushes in the garden, shadows upon shadows. Just as they reached Dermot, the figures appeared completely. They were her elderly father and her oldest son. She took two steps forward, but her father raised an arm, cautioning her to stay back.

"It's me, Dermot," said her father in the calm voice he used to settle a frightened animal. "It's only me, only Patrick, Alice's father."

Dermot pushed him away and hunkered in the darkness, the long black barrel of the rifle raised in the air, uttering an angry shout that deepened into a roar as her father shot out a hand and grabbed hold of the rifle butt.

"Dermot, listen now, it's only me, Patrick Daly. Everything is alright. Let me take the gun."

She heard the gentle authority in his voice, the sort of authority that made you agree to everything he said as though it were the most natural thing in the world. The old man knelt on one knee and placed a soothing hand on

Dermot's shoulder. A dull trance took hold of her husband's face. Carefully, her father removed the gun from his grip.

The roar of the cars diminished as they reversed back onto the road. Were their persecutors leaving because they had seen her and her father? In the darkness, she could smell the turf fires and tobacco from her father's old jacket. She drew close to his comforting presence. She expected to hear shock or fear in his voice but instead he spoke calmly. "Don't blame those stupid eejits," he said, referring to the men in the cars. "It's the past that's to blame."

The dangerous tension evaporated from Dermot's face. He remained in his crouching position, but he no longer looked as though he were crouching in enemy territory.

"What are you doing here, Patrick?" he said to his father-in-law in surprise. "And you, too?" He turned to his son with embarrassment.

"The boy woke me," said the old man. "He asked me to help. I heard the commotion and saw the lights, so I came as quickly as I could."

Alice's father was frail with wrinkled skin and an unsteady walk, but in that moment, looking at her with one hand still on Dermot's shoulder, there was something strong and youthful in his eyes.

Dermot rose, his back straight, standing slowly over the old man's stooped figure. He bid the old man goodnight and placed his arm around his son. The wind picked up and a whispering rose in the trees, a slow stirring, the trees twisting and pulling against their roots.

From the house, came the cry of their youngest daughter, calling for her mother and father.

2019

When my father called to my door, asking me to help him fell the ash tree that cast a huge shadow across their back garden, my first instinct was to say no. The only thing unique about the ash among all the other trees surrounding my parent's house was the fact that I had planted it, along with my father, shortly after the hijacking. It dominated the garden, and even though it made summer come late and autumn early, I was very fond of it. Often, I placed my cheek against its trunk and stared up at its branches, its leaves fluttering and its keys flashing in the breezes. It had been years since I'd climbed it, but I could still remember the freedom and firmness I found up there, a twenty-foot-high world with deep roots, and the plunging perspective it gave me of the family home as I leaned casually with the wind. It was a roost, a crow's nest, that allowed me to see deeper into the landscape.

I grew up in what was originally a long farmhouse, with my parents and four siblings at one end, and my widowed grandfather at the other. My father blocked off the adjoining corridor with a brick wall when we were toddlers, and then divided the house in two. Our wing of the farmhouse had extended over the years with a new two-storey block of bedrooms, a sunroom and porch, while my grandfather's wing had remained the same with its corrugated tin roof, slowly slipping into ruin after his death in 1991, making the distorted dwellings even more lob-sided. My mother was against knocking down the old house, and strangers who visited us walked around the property with a look of bemusement. But the rambling farmhouse held more truth than a brand-new building, and my grandfather's cottage, with its dark windows still intact, gave the impression that his gentle gaze remained upon us as we went about our lives in a new century. My own house, and those of my three sisters, radiated out in an arc from the central farmhouse, stretching out into the wildness of the wooded fields and little streams.

I was on the verge of protesting to my father, but I suppressed my misgivings and agreed to help him fell the tree. Looking up at it in the back of my parent's garden, I couldn't help feeling that I'd lived here too long. My father must have felt it, too. The tree blocked the evening sun, and its blackened litter of leaves and seeds choked the garden. Both of us wanted out of its shadow.

He handed me a rope, which was tied to the tree, and then he started the chainsaw. I had to step into the breach and start asking questions because it was obvious he wasn't going to give me any further instructions, and assumed I knew intuitively what he was planning to do. Which direction should I pull in? And what if the tree lurched towards the house, where my mother was watching us from the kitchen window? He made some cryptic remarks as though he were talking to himself, or the tree.

As an example of teamwork, it was a disaster. He grunted and shouted over the roar of the chainsaw, never once taking his eyes off the trunk. Now and again, he made hand signals, directing me to pull the rope from a different position in the garden, as if trees could be felled only by brute power and masculine silence.

Even though it was a cold spring day, he wore a shirt with his sleeves rolled up. It was difficult to see any signs of frailty in his body. He had lost some height and a little weight, but his stature had kept all the angles of his youth, and his shirt hugged his body as he worked. He had always been physically fit, with a sinewy strength. He and my mother rarely rose past seven and were usually outside with the early morning sun, working in their garden and polytunnels, sprightly and brisk, on good terms with nature and the landscape. They neither smoked nor drank alcohol, and their lives were still lived according to the simple, hard-working routine imbued in them as farmers' children.

Born in Monaghan, on the other side of the Irish border, my father had always been regarded as a blow-in by the rest of the parish. The fact that he was an outsider for life had placed a sort of halo around his figure, a shimmer of strangeness that allowed him to stride lightly amid his welter of grandchildren. It had helped him get through all these years living in a parish full of undercurrents circulating since the Civil War, and, more recently, the IRA hijacking and intimidation, the pools of darkness that filled and emptied.

The voices of the masked men had not reminded him of the voices of cousins or childhood friends. For my mother, their familiar accents were the weapons that had really hurt. My father enjoyed the profusion of his extended family and the ragged acres of the inherited farm, flitting from house to house with none of the responsibilities of a patriarchal landowner. That person was still my dead grandfather.

Watching him wield the chainsaw, I felt like a lightweight, an amateur house-owner and failed gardener, who lacked the gumption to tackle such a project and had no understanding at all of how to operate machinery or fell a tree. The chainsaw bit deeper into the trunk. I steadied myself and leaned back until the rope was taut. My weight and movement had little effect on the branches as they rocked in the breeze. I stared up at its crown, watching the crows, high above, riding the wind.

I'm against cutting down trees and usually wince when I see our farming neighbours machine flail or uproot their hedges with unnatural thoroughness. My grandfather never touched the many rings of thorn trees that dotted his fields. They were the ghostly settlements of wild animals and faeries. Their dark gaps always attracted me when I was a child as though they were openings to another world.

Most of the wild hedges had gone from the parish, apart from the eccentric thicket of hawthorn, blackthorn, bramble and hazel that I'd allowed to take hold like a jungle in the acre behind my house. Neglect was my chief gardening philosophy and without cows to graze and keep the undergrowth in check, new shoots sprouted from the ground every spring and invaded what were once beds of strawberries, rhubarb and fruit bushes.

The wild space behind my house has never been the type of garden that hemmed in or protected children from nature. Every summer, I crawled through it at rabbit-level with a saw and cut out long, low tunnels and little glades for our daughters and their cousins to play in and make camps. The girls came back in the evening like wild spirits with bits of moss, leaves, and dirt in their tangled hair. The thickets gave their childhood an extra edge, made their eyes dark and lively. They made potions out of sloeberries, sorrel and wildflowers, and when Frances and I settled them into bed at night, they gave us wild looks and dark smiles as though they were secretly planning to run away.

The cutting roar of the chainsaw intensified against the softer roar of the tree's foliage. The ash's summit creaked, and then it fell with an immense crack, yanking me several feet into the air. Its branches flared out across the garden and bits of bark, seeds and leaves, rained down upon us. The collapsed canopy filled the garden and was lit up by fresh sprees of sunlight. My father and I stepped over the branches and stared at the rings of the tree stump.

"There it is," he said with a grin of triumph. "The past. All the way back to 1982."

We counted the innermost rings, the first summer after the hijacking, engraved in the tree's heart, and the following summers radiating out like a ripple, spreading and shading into each other. My father started up the saw again and began cutting off the branches. He grew chattier, made little jokes and smiled as we heaved the branches out of the way. The ice had been broken.

"Good job you had two eggs for breakfast this morning," he said.

The smell of diesel, smoke and wood-dust filled the air, and something else, my father's elderly machismo, his silvery poise, the same machismo that had made him confront the IRA in the middle of the night with a double-barrelled shotgun, a strict and elemental man who was prepared to use the power of a mechanism when necessary, the trigger of a gun or a chain-saw cord.

It struck me that if it had been his father who'd been arrested by the police, if it had been his neighbours who hijacked the car, he would have explained everything to me while planting and felling this tree, and the story would have turned into an anecdote or cautionary tale rolled smooth by time. A story I might have taken little notice of, a story without the aura of secrecy that hung over my mother's side of the family. My father's stories left no room for the imagination. They were too real to write about, too easy to conceive. They lacked the danger of opening a Pandora's Box.

I turned to glance at my mother, who was still working at the kitchen sink. Her head was down, and she didn't glance up to watch what we were doing, which was unlike her. I had set up my home next to her and my father's house. She and her past and its stories were going to be there forever, forming part of my story and my children's in this landscape that was not my landscape but ours, or perhaps just my mother and grandfather's because they were the only ones who had lived here authentically. I lifted my arm and waved over at the window, but still she didn't look up.

"How's the book about Diseart coming along?" asked my father.

"How do you know I'm writing a book about Diseart?"

"We all know," he said with a smile. "None of us can keep a secret here." He meant it as a joke but when he saw the look on my face he stopped. "Your mum told me."

My extended family and I belonged to a see-through landscape, the walls of our snug homes, nestled together in this hollow, may as well have been made of glass.

"Have you nearly finished it?" he asked.

"Far from it. I'm stuck in the middle." Suddenly I felt as though I were defending myself. "It'll probably take forever and then never see the light of day."

"Forever is a long time," he replied. He had lived in Diseart for over forty years but had never lost the soft lilt of his Monaghan accent. His tone was relaxed, but then his voice lowered. "Your mother wants to talk to you about your book."

His hand slid from the branch we were holding and patted me on the shoulder, turning me in the right direction. She was waiting for me at the window. When he had deftly steered me towards her, he slipped away into

131

the garden.

My mother had opened all the windows in the house and the spring air rushed in yet there was a heavy atmosphere in the kitchen. Perhaps it was the effect of moving from the warm spring sunshine. I felt the sudden coldness on my skin and hesitated on the doorstep. She kept working at the sink, and an eternity seemed to pass without either of us saying anything. Unlike my father, my mother could never tolerate silences, and it was highly unlikely her work at the sink was keeping her from speaking.

I asked her a question about the old days, what sort of wood did her father store and season for firewood? Would he have used ash or beech or hazel? The silence continued and I felt the brooding atmosphere of the room take hold. We were too similar, she and I, and our silences were a thing to dread.

"I'm not going to answer any more questions about the past," she said without looking up from the sink.

She turned and walked into the living room.

"How did you find out I was writing about Diseart?" I asked, following her.

"You've been behaving oddly. Asking all sorts of questions about the past."

"I'm surprised you noticed." Suddenly it wasn't guilt that I felt, but a familiar resentment.

"Your sister and I noticed all right. I could tell that something was brewing in you on Station Island. Something strange."

"What do you mean?"

"The way you kept talking about the hijacking and Donaghy's murder. It's my fault I suppose. I should have warned you back then."

A spark of anger rose in me, but I quelled it. What

mattered was the story and now she had brought it up, I had an opportunity to ask her questions about the fourth member of the IRA gang. But as soon as I mentioned the hijacking, her face immediately froze, and she refused to tell me anything.

"But what about the effect on you and dad, the mental and emotional scars. Surely, that needs to be talked about some day?"

"Scars like that can heal on their own. All your dad and I wanted was peace to get on with our lives." She stared at me firmly. "Certain things should stay secret. Promise me you won't go round asking questions about the IRA hijackers. Especially the one who wasn't killed."

"Why? Is it a secret?"

"I told you, somethings are better not talked about."

But his identity could not remain secret anymore. My story would not give me back my life without answers to the questions I had raised. The truth had to be told. My mother's silence would have to be betrayed, even though I might have to pay a price someday.

"I've already talked to Malachy Warde about him."

She sat down in her usual armchair.

"Did you now?"

"And I got the strangest of responses. At first, he was reluctant to tell me his name, and then he told me it was a man called Dominic Hughes from Cloghgar."

"Malachy...told you that?"

"Yes. I went straight up to the graveyard in Cloghgar and found his headstone. But the strange thing was it said Hughes died in 1981. He can't have been the fourth IRA man. There must be some reason why Warde is keeping his name secret."

"What are you trying to get out of this?"

At the start, it had been a grubby wish. To have a

publisher commission a book that wasn't a standard crime novel and bolster my ego. I who had waited all these years before renouncing the comfortable clichés of detective fiction. But in researching and writing the novel, my perspective had changed.

"Yesterday, when I was in Cloghgar graveyard, it crossed my mind that I might be meant to play the role of detective. And work out the missing elements of the story."

"Detective stories, that's what we're talking about here, isn't it?"

"Yes, you're right." Part of me was prepared to give in to her line of questioning so that I could quickly escape. I wanted to surrender myself to that other world that was waiting for me, the world of my writing.

"I don't like interfering but I'm worried," she said.

"About what?"

"How do you intend to find out his name. Are you going to confront the IRA?"

"I don't know. I don't plan to confront them, but I have questions for them."

My mother was silent. I had been leaning against the side of the sofa, and now straightened up to signal that I intended the conversation to end, but my mother didn't move. She had a fixed look on her face, one that suggested the conversation was far from over and would go on during the night until dawn if necessary.

"I'm no expert on writing books, but I don't see how you can be so sure there's a mystery to solve. The fourth IRA man could be anyone in the parish. If that particular man hadn't been there, it would have been someone else, his brother, his cousin, his neighbour. It's all the same when you're hiding behind a balaclava."

My mother stared at me and frowned. I should not have delayed. I should not have explained what the story was about or entered the kitchen door in the first place.

"Am I in this story?" she asked.

"Yes – you, me, dad, your father. We're all in it."

"When can I read it?"

"When it's finished."

"Will it upset me?"

"I hope not."

"You hope not?"

My adrenaline levels began to rise. How easy it would have been to cover my tracks and pretend the book had turned into another crime novel, albeit one that was so accurate, so exactly right in the descriptions of our family life that it read more like a memoir, or a true crime story.

I described some of the conversations and incidents that I had written, and she looked at me as though she could not believe her ears. The more I described what I had written, the more it sounded as though I had been sleuthing round her house like an amateur detective, butting in on her family research, hunting through her memorabilia and her past, taking over conversations and family stories in order to advance the plot of my book.

Brusquely, she asked, "Does Frances know what you're doing?"

"Yes."

"Is she in the book?"

"I've told you already. We're all in it."

My grandfather's blood had started the story, and I wanted to believe that it had set in chain a course of events, the death of his uncle, and much later, the hijacking of our car and the murder of a policeman. I had created a puzzle out of my grandfather's handkerchief, a passport photo of his uncle and the gold-coloured bullet the IRA had handed me, and now I stood before the one living person who might remember and help me solve the puzzle, but wouldn't, because she was my mother and didn't trust me. It was too late to pretend that I could approach the past like an historian, or a fact-obsessed journalist. I was someone who made up things, who wrote about clues and questions, and was seeking to reinforce his suspicions.

"You know what I think?" she said. "Writing about your family is the same as hijacking them. Holding them at gunpoint with your pen."

"You're probably right. I'm forcing us to confront the things we've ignored. To see the past in ways we wouldn't otherwise."

"You're being very mysterious. What exactly are you talking about?"

Frustration at being shut away alone with the story for months began to bubble up.

"The truth," I said.

She clicked her tongue. "You told me on Station Island that writers were professional liars. I don't think you're interested in the truth at all."

I didn't answer. Sometimes it didn't matter whether it was a lie or a truth. It was all a question of what the reader felt in their heart, what memories and feelings were evoked. Sometimes a lie could bring readers closer to the emotional truth.

"Why don't you and Frances come up for dinner this evening," she said. "We can talk about other stories. Let's get you back to writing about your detective Celcius Daly. And no more questions about the hijacking."

"But I don't have a choice anymore."

Her eyes filled with annoyance.

"What do you mean?"

"I have to keep asking questions and finish this story. I can't destroy all that I've worked on."

"I'm not asking you to destroy anything." She sighed. "You have to do what you think is best."

I tried to explain to her that in starting the story, I felt obliged to finish it, that beginning it had been a long journey and the ideas had been percolating in my mind for years. I was afraid my writer's block would continue indefinitely and that I'd float around in a state of pseudo-employment, teaching creative-writing here and there, talking about my crime novels to anyone who could be bothered to listen, frozen by doubt and a lack of will to write the book that I really wanted to write, the book that was in me and in the landscape that I had made my home. I couldn't let future regrets paralyse me, fearing the consequences of a story that I had not yet written, and would probably never be published anyway. I felt dutybound to keep telling the story by the people who were no longer alive, my grandfather, his uncle, Tom Donaghy and Ivan White. The past compelled me to keep writing, my own frustrations compelled me, the miserable history of our tribe in this parish of bog and moor compelled me. The part of the story I knew nothing about compelled me, the ending of the story that still lay beyond my comprehension.

As I spoke, she stared at the floor, her hands resting on her knees, her mouth crooked in a frown of concentration. I wished my father were here. He would have nodded and wished me good luck with the book, and only afterwards, in private, would he have mulled over the consequences.

"I still don't understand. Why do you need to include us in the story?"

"Because without you I would never be capable of writing it. I would have filled pages every day but none of it would have been any good."

"I take it you're happy with what you've written?"

"Yes."

"Well then, I'm pleased to have been useful."

"More than useful."

I stood up to go, but she came up with more questions to delay me.

"Why write about the hijacking and your grandfather? Why not make something up?"

I shrugged. "I've asked myself that question every day for the past six months."

It wasn't that it was an easier story to write. I'd expended twice as much time and emotional energy trying to write a true story as making up a fiction. I was tied to my mother and her father. The intimacy I felt was immense and the empathy between us overwhelming. The writer in me wanted to scrutinise that, to find the pain and beauty in it. This was the most important thing I would ever write about, and I didn't want to make a mess of it. Every day my duties and routine as a husband and parent overlapped with those of a son and brother, the different roles always competing with and subordinating each other. And the longing for something more meaningful and adventurous sometimes undermined my efforts to be a good father and a good son. Happiness lay somewhere else, I selfishly thought, in knowing that I was in charge of my own life and free to choose.

"You care more about your book than about us," she said.

"That's not true."

Silence. Her gaze didn't change.

In spite of my mother's disapproval, I suppressed the

feelings of guilt. She sat and frowned at me, but I felt nothing. I looked at her. Our discussion was over. Her judgement had been made and I felt empty inside. Before I had become obsessed with writing this book, the sight of any displeasure on my mother or father's face would have upset me and disturbed the creative flow. A small shadow of anxiety fell across my thoughts. Had I escaped that filial guilt forever? And if so, would I ever be able to write about it again?

"There isn't much more to say," she said.

I wanted to place my hand on her shoulder and reassure her that I was her son and would always protect her and never abandon her, but in reaching out to her I was also clinging to her. I was still a child in her eyes, albeit one who was as old as her father had been when she was a little girl. The feeling I had was that this world I shared with my extended family in Diseart was too small and too tightly enclosed, and the only opening I had was through writing, and even that was doomed to fail. Writing about my family's past was like slowly tugging out a roll of barbed wire from the ground. I thought of saying sorry, there and then, but I sensed an apology would irritate her. Instead, I would have to keep telling the story, and put up with the consequences, as a grown-up writer should.

I nodded and walked out through the back door. The moon had risen in the evening sky and now fell clearly across the garden. There was a new sharpness in the air, an illuminated emptiness where the fallen ash tree lay.

1982

The following morning, Dermot walked to the bottom of the driveway and removed the cattle grid from the entrance. A gaping hole now awaited his tormentors if they tried to drive up to his house again. Afterwards, he cleaned his shotgun, oiled it, bought a fresh set of cartridges and placed it next to his bedside locker.

He had never been a vindictive person. He had never actively sought revenge against another human being, but these IRA men, even though they were his neighbours, no longer belonged to the normal category of human beings. They were murderers and he wanted them caught and punished. They were dangerous to all law-abiding Catholics who held to the certainties of family and faith. They deserved retribution, to do some form of penance. They had decided Ivan White should be put to his death, and in doing so they had placed an intolerable burden on Dermot's family, turning them into guilty bystanders, grilled by the police, harassed by the British Army, suffering all the rigours of a drawn-out investigation.

He was thirty-five, in the middle of his life, and the thought of the danger he was in made his heart ache. The spring sunlight filled the garden, giving him a vision of clarity. The fields of his father-in-law's farm had changed. He had never grasped their wildness before or was it that the whitethorn and gorse bushes had slowly taken over now that his father-in-law was growing infirm and unable to cut and burn them every year? The marshy hollows and springs were filled with weeds rotting into a dark green slime. Every evening, his children came back after playing in the thickets, covered in scrapes, cuts and hurts. The thorns he squeezed from their little hands seemed like attacks on life and the blood flowed easily from the thorn pricks.

He read somewhere that you should plant a tree before you die. He imagined the scrub fields beyond the garden cleared of gorse, bushes, brambles and rushes, and planted with young trees. The vision gave him a strange lift and calmed his thoughts. He imagined his home enclosed by a forest, the trees surging upwards, fed by hidden springs, his five children growing up, tall, strong and healthy amid hazel, beech and oak trees. They would breathe in the leaf-purified air, pick their way under swaying branches through the sun-dappled shade, leaving behind all the dark things of the Troubles.

With his eldest son, he planted the first tree, an ash sapling from his mother's farm in Monaghan. It felt like he was starting a journey, creating a path for his family into the future. In the following days, he planted the fields around the house with more saplings, each tree representing what he wanted to be in the future, permanent, rooted, watching over and protecting his children. But he was an outsider, trapped in a conspiracy of silence and a shadow hung over his future in the parish. He dug and planted each tree out of blind instinct. He smelt the fragrance of freshly dug soil. He wandered amid the whips of hazel and beech, firming the soil with his boots. He understood that the well of life was inexhaustible, but still the worry was there, the sadness that he might not see his children grow up.

Nevertheless. he made his decision and drove into town, parked his car and marched up to the first payphone. He was surprised by his determination. Even though he understood that in punishing the IRA he would also be punishing himself and his family, he pushed on with his plans. He had postponed this moment for long enough, had done everything he could to avoid it, but now he had no choice but to face up to his responsibilities. Deep down, he knew it would always come to this. He dropped several coins into the slot and rang the number Murphy gave him. The detective answered on the fifth ring. The pleasurable surprise in Murphy's voice was unmistakeable.

2019

What was I doing writing a story that was anchoring me more heavily in the past, tying me down to a god-forsaken parish at the bottom of a bleak mountain? I should be writing about my mother and grandfather as children, with worlds and lives that were still full of dreams and possible futures that hadn't been fully realised or lost. I needed stories that would help me float and take me by surprise into unknown worlds, rather than weigh me down. But now that I had found this story full of secrets, I was determined to finish it.

I spent the next fortnight avoiding my parents and sisters as much as possible. I did everything I could to keep them at arm's length. If the doorbell rang, I ignored it and waited for the sound of footsteps to die along the lane. I didn't pick up the phone. I immersed myself in the daily drill of school runs, teaching creative writing, cooking and cleaning the house. I didn't want to remember the way my mother's eyes stared right through me. I spent my mornings teaching in local colleges, or jogging through the forests of the Sperrin Mountains, tramping along paths at the edges of rivers, my head full of the restless dynamics of writing. I tried not to think about my new novel, but it was impossible.

It had been a wet spring, and I trod the ground into a quagmire. The rivers were in full spate and ate away at the paths. I felt appalled by the coldness in my heart and my compulsion to keep writing. I berated myself for tormenting my mother about the past, but somehow, I needed to keep writing to keep my distance from her love.

In my head, I kept changing the novel's meandering plot, opening gaps in the story, while my feet pounded the eroding paths. It felt as though everything was slipping into ruin, my loss of filial compassion, and my story's loss of direction and substance. Jogging for miles had always been my favourite form of escape, the only time when I felt truly alone and answerable to no one, but the more I ran the more I felt like a prisoner trapped in a circle, and at the centre of it was the story of the hijacking and the identity of the fourth IRA man. I was torn between the necessity of writing it and the impossibility of writing it.

How had my writing brought me to this never-ending cycle of guilt? I should be forging a world beyond the story of my family, beyond the grasp and influence of the past. I loved my parents and sisters, but I lived too close to them, and without the buffer of Frances and my children I would have been smothered by my mother's tender, worried, controlling presence. I was two-faced, a writer and a son, and could do little else but wallow in the guilt of my double-life.

I kept running every day, running to leave behind the past, but never running far enough to escape it. Was there anything that could get me out of this bind? Some sort of natural disaster might, striking our home, or perhaps an accidental fire, burning my notebooks to ashes and forcing us to move to another part of the country.

One morning, I forced my feet into an old pair of Wellington boots, grabbed a spade and spent the rest of the day maniacally digging the back field. I sliced through roots and worms, grunting as I heaved the wet clay and fashioned it into potato drills. If only I could take the sharp edge of the spade to the past. Somehow, I had to earn the right to be invited into my grandfather's world. Only then, would I be able to uncover its secrets.

But what if the past never opened up to me? What if I was never able to finish the story? My grandfather had planted potatoes for years in the ground I was now digging, and I could picture his lean stooping figure, his Herculean digging prowess. What would he have to say about my writing? Every sod of earth in this field of his was telling me something, chiding me for my lack of contentment and stillness, warning me that it was the time to stop writing stories, that my life was slowly disappearing away because my thoughts were always somewhere else. The world of my stories had expanded at the expense of my family life and my peace of mind.

Through the thorn trees and the drifting rags of rain clouds there hung a light that resembled the light of holy pictures, and I suddenly thought I understood how my grandfather was able to absorb the epiphanies of his faith into the fabric of his daily life. As he dug the potato drills on this headland, not lifting his eyes once from the rows of clay, he was rooting himself to the spot, but also to eternity. His boots were weighed down with lumps of mud, but he was always floating when he worked in these fields. The underground springs floated the entire headland, the marshy meadows, the cottages and the church, carrying them towards some distant shore.

The afternoon grew gloomy, and a storm set in. Rain swept across the fields and fell heavily. I kept digging, dredging the ground for meaning and memories. I straightened up and listened to the wind roaring through the blackthorn thickets. The sounds rose sharply. I felt exhilarated by the freshness of the storm in the midst of home and the web of family. I forced to myself to keep digging against the wind, imagining that I was riding the crest of a great wave, my spade a paddle. The rain receded and the last of the gale exploded the sunset sky into pulses of ragged light, purple and red clouds streaming east.

Adventure and exhilaration could happen anywhere, just as freedom could be at its wildest in the shadow of home. Amid the strange crying and whining noises of a blackthorn hedge, a grandson might find a listening post more meaningful than a snug study lined with books. I kept digging, thinking of the warm house that would soon greet me and the prospect of writing in the long hours to dawn. The storm had reconciled me with the landscape, and later, on an empty page, I would try to bring it home.

In the watery dusk, I enjoyed striding the field, contemplating the freshly dug ground and staring through the thorns at the parish church as it shone palely on the hill. And when I walked back to the house, I felt a deep tiredness in the core of my being, completely different and more satisfying than the emotional tiredness I got from writing. My exhaustion was purest out there, digging long into the twilight, a place where I was invisible and anonymous. Invigorated and full of the raw air of spring, I stepped into the house and gave Frances a sweeping kiss as she stood in the kitchen. My lips must have felt cold and rough to her, but she just smiled and looked at me strangely.

My mind settled around the ache in my back, and I slept soundly. This was life, the life of the land. This was the whole wide world shrunk to an acre of scutch grass, blackthorn stumps and nettles. My body was wakening from a drugged existence.

1982

The silence in the middle of the night woke Dermot to an informer's instant fear. He opened his eyes and stared at the ceiling, listening for the sound of their IRA tormentors but heard nothing. Somehow the lack of noise seemed more intimidating. He felt Alice stir beside him, her body turning away from his, but when he leant over and peered at her, she was deep in sleep. The questions he wanted to ask her, her links to the masked men who'd emerged from the hedge and the secrets between her and her neighbours tumbled through his mind in a spin dryer of confused suspicions. He rose, walked downstairs and opened the back door. The temperature had dropped and even though it was early April, a light snow fell through the darkness. He stood transfixed by the sight of snowflakes drifting out of the blackness. He had the odd sensation that winter had somehow sniffed him out. The flakes planted themselves on his bare feet, marking their target, and then they swarmed over his pyjamas.

He heard footsteps behind. Alice crossed the floor and joined him at the doorstep where a shadow of snow had settled. It was a night for comfort and shelter, hunkering around the hearth or deep under blankets.

"Aren't you cold?" she said.

"Yes, I am."

The rawness of the air, their hushed voices and the late hour combined to give him a sense of looming danger.

"I talked to Murphy. Described what I saw of their faces."

"I thought you would."

"Murphy says there's still not enough evidence to convict anyone. That's all there is to it."

"A clear conscience, then?"

"A clear conscience. I've done what I think is right."

"Then we don't need to talk about it anymore."

"Yes."

For several days, they adhered steadfastly to the code of silence. They did not talk about Murphy, the IRA or their neighbours. Slowly, Dermot began to feel less alone, and his wife and neighbours begin to resemble the people they were before the hijacking.

Late one night, Murphy called, unannounced, just after the children's bedtime. Dermot opened the door and nodded curtly at the detective.

"I've been trying to phone you all evening," said Murphy gravely. He stepped into the hall.

"We were out," lied Dermot.

"Something unexpected has come up. An important development."

"Can't it wait?"

Murphy raised his eyebrows, whether to plead or warn, it was difficult to tell. "I'm sorry, it can't."

The detective explained that a serious error had been made. The prosecuting council had prepared an evidence file for one of the IRA suspect's solicitors and mistakenly included Dermot's address in a footnote, linking him to the only witness testimony in the file.

After a pause, Dermot asked, "Who's to blame..." His voice sounded far-off, detached from his thoughts. He stood there, staring at Murphy. How would the IRA react to the discovery? What would they do to him in retaliation?

Murphy shrugged his shoulders awkwardly. "It's not really something I can discuss," he said with a frown.

Dermot met his look with one of his own. "You can't throw me to the wolves like that."

"Of course not." Murphy promised him round the clock protection, even relocation to a safe house, if he wanted it. "Look, there are things I have to follow up. If you need to, you can ring me at any time." Murphy gave Dermot a nod and left quickly.

With an effort, Dermot shoved the front door closed. He leaned his forehead against the cold glass and breathed. The taillights of the detective's car vanished into the night. He tried to work out the implications of what Murphy had told him. He closed his eyes. The sick feeling of being one of the fallen, a shameful informer, filled his stomach. A touch on his shoulder made him turn around. The smooth face of Alice, framed by her long dark hair, stared at him.

"What's wrong?"

"I'm all right."

"You don't look all right."

"I'm okay."

"Do you want a cup of tea? Some supper?"

"No. But we need to talk."

He explained to her what Murphy had said. He spoke in an agitated voice, as though it wasn't really Alice he was speaking to in the dimly lit hall, but one of their shadowy neighbours.

She told him to calm down. She held his hand and stared at him with a look of utmost conviction and set forth her plan on how they would get through the next few weeks to the court case, which, she said, would surely collapse because of a lack of evidence. He didn't have to stand over anything he had told the police. He could retract everything and cite witness intimidation as a reason for withdrawing his evidence.

"Do you hear me, Dermot," she said. "Am I right or am I wrong?"

He watched her as she rose and removed a bottle of whiskey from a cupboard. He weighed up his choices. He promised himself on the day of his marriage that he would lead his life as a good husband and father, a moral human being. He wanted to do the right thing, to be a brave and honourable citizen, but as his wife put the glass of whiskey before him and placed her hand on his shoulder, his conviction faltered. He told himself that being caught in a war between the IRA and the police was not a moral issue. The survival of his family was not a moral issue. It was a biological imperative, and in order to keep his wedding vows, his words and actions must bring no harm to his home and children.

He told her she was right. He had no other choice. The sip of the whiskey, the first in years, left a sweet tingle in his throat. The next morning, he rang his solicitor and instructed him that he was withdrawing his testimony due to IRA intimidation.

However, the night-time persecution increased and the soldiers' behaviour at the checkpoints grew nastier, their roadside waits longer and more oppressive. A date was set for the first hearing of the court-case, April 19th, two weeks away.

2019

"Did I wake you?" said the voice at the other end of the phone line. It was an old man's voice, cracking slightly.

"No," I replied.

"Good. I remember you said you got up early to write. I was awake already and thought we'd better get started."

"Who is this?"

"I can't answer that right now, but I'll give you some clues to help prod your memory. Here's one, I drive an old green Renault."

My mind drew a blank. "I don't know you."

"You might not remember me, but you definitely do know me. And so do your readers." He spoke so slowly and with such confidence that I could do nothing but hold the phone tighter to my ear as if I might somehow narrow the distance between us.

"I'm sorry, I don't you know at all," I said and put the phone down.

Who on earth would be ringing me at half six in the morning and playing such strange games? My mind wandered to the news reports I had written involving local criminals and undesirable characters. A journalist inevitably made many enemies. Was the mysterious caller intent on harassing me for something I had written in the past? Disorientated, annoyed, I looked around the silent hallway. The house at this time of the day was my refuge, quiet and secure, and I resented any form of intrusion.

I took a shower to rinse away the anxious speculation. Afterwards, I went down to the kitchen to make myself some porridge and toast. I had risen before five and almost finished my daily quota of words. The girls and Frances were still sleeping, and it was too early to do anything else. But my mother and father would be up. They'd be having breakfast or pottering around their garden in the dawn light.

At first, it felt like an impulse. The longing to hear my parents' voices. It had been a fortnight since I'd spoken to them. There was no explanation other than love that made me walk outside and stare at the tree-lined path joining our houses. The sun had risen high enough to create an interplay of light and darkness through the beech and hazel trees, and the path shone with the early morning dew. I could resist its invitation no longer. In a strange way, I felt at peace with the strong currents that tugged me onward.

I knew that the rift between my mother and I was temporary, and that sooner rather than later we would work out a way to continue living together in Diseart, in this ark of households she had drawn together on the farm she'd inherited from her father. The currents of belonging flowed between our separate households, forces that didn't carry us away in our lives, but brought us deeper, absorbing us in the unending conversations and concealments of our lives. Sometimes, we all did and said things that left another member of the family feeling perplexed or angry. Some days we went over in our heads a conversation or dim memory that everyone else had forgotten completely but nevertheless exercised an undue influence over our thoughts and behaviour. We were like fragile boats pulled apart by equal and opposite forces and there was no way of knowing what another member of the family felt or how they would react from one day to another.

It had rained all spring; the rivers were rivers again

and there was flooding, but it was more than water that rose and bubbled underground. Memories and the worlds of my childhood, my mother's and grandfather's overflowed and became palpable in the landscape. Living in this familiar world was the best thing that could have happened to me as a father and husband, and as a writer, too. I could never move my children to another part of the country, even though I sometimes felt we had run out of time living together as an extended family. For one thing, our daughters would have protested too fiercely.

Little did I know, as I walked up the path, that ahead of me everything was gathering in one current and advancing towards a waterfall.

I found my mother in the kitchen. She was standing over the gas stove, watching the pans as she cooked breakfast. Something lurched inside me. She looked older than when we had last spoken, and frailer. The total of her years felt like a widening gulf between us. But the voice that greeted me was strong and full of warmth.

"How are Frances and the children?" she asked. Her hands moved over the pans, flipping pancakes, turning bacon, and stirring the porridge.

"Couldn't be better. The girls are playing in the school orchestra on Thursday night. You and dad can come along, if you want."

"That sounds lovely. And what about you?"

"Keeping busy."

She averted her face suddenly.

"Busy writing?"

"Yes. Busy writing."

"I'm glad you're over your writer's block."

"I hope so."

We had safely crossed an invisible boundary. On one side was a writer and his subjects; on the other was a son and mother. We both wanted to remain on the mother and son side of the line. Otherwise, the tenderness and trust in our relationship would have ended, or changed into something else, which was not what either of us wanted. I didn't say anything more. I was worried I might accidentally cross that tentative boundary.

She started telling me a story about her grandmother that I had never heard before. That she should greet me with a smile and open up about her past was more than I could have hoped for. Perhaps she would give me her blessing after all. But something interrupted the telling. Something that seemed to diminish her, not her physical body but her aura, the waves of vitality she emitted and which made her presence always palpable as soon as you entered her house, even if you couldn't see or hear her. The smile never left her lips, but her mouth was twisted, and she stopped speaking. She dropped the spoon in the porridge, stumbled and lost her balance.

"What's wrong?" I asked, reaching out to help and steady her.

The pot of porridge overflowed and puddled on the hob. She grabbed my arm. I could feel her body failing her, leaning into mine. Her grey hair was matted with sweat. Briefly, she rallied. Her strength returned and I was able to help her walk slowly into the sitting room.

I went to open a window, telling her that a bit of fresh air might be a good idea, but I was fooling myself. I got her a glass of water, but she was unable to sip it. A horrible knot seemed to be twisting through her body.

"What's wrong?" I asked again.

She leaned into the armchair and struggled to breathe. A mistiness settled in her eyes. Something was badly wrong. "I'm not well," she whispered.

In an even weaker voice, she asked me to get the blood

pressure monitor. With a limp hand she wrapped the cuff around her arm and tightened it. Her movements were slow. Her body seemed to struggle as she ordered her arm, her hand, her fingers to perform the familiar operation. I moved to help her, but she frowned. She had been taking patients' blood pressure readings all her life and could do it in her sleep, and now she took her own reading with a measured calm.

She stared at the digital screen with shadowed eyes. The two of us listened to the beeps of the machine and then a set of numbers flashed up. She contemplated them for a moment and sighed. "74 over 30, pulse 180," she said. "Phone the ambulance."

I rang 999, gave our address and a quick history of my mother's symptoms. The operator told me an ambulance would be along soon, and to make sure the way was unobstructed for the paramedics.

When I returned to my mother, another wave of weakness overcame her, and her face grew lined and grey. She clutched my hand. I tried to calm her by holding her hand and talking to her, but she didn't seem to hear. Her eyes opened and she came round. She gave me a little nod and attempted to smile.

We sat there next to the table of memorabilia and waited for the ambulance. I only wanted to remember in this room, to do what I always did, to sit in her company and guess the past. I didn't want to contemplate or foresee what might happen in the future. She whispered to me something about the family will. I reassured her, told her to breathe slowly and deeply. I heard my calm voice, my soothing words in the quiet room. She told me her symptoms, the band of pain across her chest, the nausea and the feeling that she was about to lose consciousness, so that I could relay them to the paramedics.

There was a shout from the door and then my father appeared. He tried to take her hand, but she dismissed him with a frown and held onto mine. There were more voices and hurried movements. My sisters arrived with frantic eyes. My mother and I stayed calm as they packed a hospital bag, assembled her tablets and wrote out a list of medicines to which she was allergic. I talked to her in a reassuring voice and felt a twinge of relief that she and I were composed. I had behaved so fearfully in the past and was glad that I had convinced her we could be brave together. She sat quietly with half-open eyes, detaching herself from the scene she was causing, not wanting to make any trouble for anyone, and although I could see the fear in my father's and sisters' eyes, they did their best to temper their emotions, conversing in whispers and moving swiftly but soundlessly, not wanting to cause any disturbance either.

I felt her grip strengthen. I thought I glimpsed a shadow of a smile, a fleeting expression on her face. Was it a flash of resignation? No. The gesture strengthened. She was recovering. She smiled with ease now. A vital energy returned to her face, but the glow of relief in her eyes seemed completely unconnected to what was happening around her, the abandoned breakfast dishes, the blood pressure monitor, and my father and sisters preparing for the arrival of the ambulance.

I was her son, obedient and waiting with her. I was good at waiting. Did I think she might not recover? No, I didn't even consider the possibility. Everything about my mother, her stories, her garden, her cooking, her passion for family history and Diseart itself, bubbled with life and lightness. There was always a dozen things she had to do, and her joy and enthusiasm added a gloss to everything she did, even the most mundane tasks such as bringing her grandchildren to school, calling on a poorly neighbour or weeding her rows of blueberries and blackcurrants. Did I really think her energy and drive would endure long into old age? Yes, I did.

The French doors flung open, and the figures of the paramedics appeared, razor sharp, lit by the spring sunshine. Their footsteps on the thick carpet were soundless. One of them carried a machine with lots of wires. My mother lowered her eyelids. The sudden movement seemed to fatigue and confuse her.

The paramedic peered at my mother, trying to get a better look at her face. "I was here last year, wasn't I," she said cheerfully.

My mother looked up at her. "Yes. You're Katey. From Eglish."

"That's right."

My mother turned terribly pale again and was too weak to say anything else. Her eyes opened and fixed on mine. She was entrusting herself to me and my account. I spoke on her behalf, relaying the history she had given me, describing carefully how the attack came on as she was cooking breakfast.

"The last time we took your mother to hospital, what happened?"

Confusion took hold of me. "What do you mean?"

"What did the cardiac consultant say? What did the tests show?"

My mother was the type of person who defied doctors and shunned hospitals. Lying in bed killed old people, she often said. The body had to be kept moving. And then it came back to me. A strange, suspended memory of last spring, my mother in a hospital bed, dressed in a flowery new dressing gown, her head propped on pillows. Yes, she had been brought to hospital in an ambulance, but it had been a minor scare. She'd discharged herself before the doctors could do any testing. She hadn't been like the other patients on the ward, the old ladies shrivelled to nothing under white sheets. But she had been on the cardiac ward, so the doctors must have believed her condition was heart related. The paramedic was right. It was this time last year. And hadn't there been another emergency the year before that, another visit to the hospital with the same symptoms.

"I'm sorry; I can't remember," I said, feeling as though I was defending myself and my mother.

"How has your mother been before this morning?" asked the paramedic.

"In fantastic health. She never stops. She was cooking away with four or five pans when I called up."

My mother gave a wan frown, and my youngest sister, Edel, interrupted. "She's been very unwell," said my sister, and proceeded to give a list of my mother's ailments and recent medical appointments, which gave the impression that nearly every major organ in her body was in a state of near collapse. My mother closed her eyes as if sealing the truth of my sister's account. Her body was exhausted. With increased urgency, my sister rattled through the medication she was on.

How could I have deceived myself that she was fit and in good health? How could I have been so indifferent to her true physical condition? Somehow, I had lost the ability to pay close attention to the truth, the warning signs of fatigue and dizziness that she frequently mentioned, the evenings when she sat collapsed in an armchair. I said no more to the paramedic after that. I had revealed too much already.

The paramedics paid more attention to my sister and things started to move swiftly. My mother didn't react as they hooked her up to the monitor. She sat there, head down, staring deep into herself. A chill went down my spine.

They measured her blood pressure and oxygen levels. The flickering screens were filled with lines and numbers, and the machine began to spew a print-out of her heart reading. Edel, a cardiac nurse, examined it, lifting it gently in the air, as though she were holding the disappearing traces of my mother's destiny, the lifeline she had been born with and that had carried her in waves through pain and joy, good fortune and bad, an undulating journey that no book could ever travel or chart. I hoped that my mother's lines were still strong, and weren't about to wear out, just yet. The paramedics gave her oxygen, and she took deep breaths. I could feel the warmth return to her hand and, in her eyes, I saw a look of relief as they lifted her into a wheelchair.

Seldom do we get enough warnings in life, or gentle reminders. When the waterfall looms ahead it is already too late to turn back, and the little time we have together is the final gift from fate. When the ambulance took my mother away, speeding soundlessly down the road, lights flashing, I grew afraid.

1982

A familiar car pulled up on the road outside the house, and shortly afterwards a shadow appeared in the porch. Dermot recognised Murphy at once, even though he could only partially see him in the darkness - the detective's familiar stoop and way of waiting, unmistakeable in time or place, the same stoop when Murphy had waited in line to be slapped by the headmaster, and which made him, this evening, resemble a forlorn lover, watching and waiting for Dermot to open the door. Did the detective know that Alice had just switched off the kitchen light and gone to bed?

Dermot located the front door key in the sideboard and made a special effort not to appear angry when he opened the door.

"I've just called to let you know I won't need to see you again, Dermot," said Murphy. "The court-case has collapsed, and the investigation has been halted. The IRA men who hijacked your car will never be prosecuted."

Dermot froze. He could hardly believe his ears. Was Murphy letting him off the hook? Had the detective conceded defeat in bringing the IRA men to justice? For the past few months, Murphy had seemed burdened by the interrogation, the repetitive questions and lurking suspicions. Dermot had thought Murphy was destined to keep asking the same questions day after day, making promises and encouragements, informing him of troubling developments, probing his silences, listening and waiting for some sort of breakthrough.

Murphy shrugged. "There's nothing more the police

can do. Worry no more about the court case, Dermot. It's out of our hands now."

Dermot propped himself against the door frame. "But someone needs to finish things," he said. There had to be some form of conclusion, a resolution that would put everyone in their rightful places, the killers, the guilty bystanders and the victims. He stared at Murphy's lowered head and hidden eyes.

"Sometimes, all we can do is try," said the detective. "The effort of bringing these killers to justice is enough. To get a glimpse of their faces beneath the masks. Tomorrow, I'll have a new investigation, a new set of killers to find. More leads and clues to follow. With luck they'll be enough to keep me going." He stared at Dermot. "What happens to the IRA gang is no longer our concern."

Dermot reflected on whether it was or wasn't. Perhaps the detective was right.

Murphy repeated a gesture and phrase Dermot had once employed in response to one of the detective's questions. He waved a casual hand towards the dark mountain. "The truth lies out there." Awkwardly, he extended his hand. "Goodbye, Dermot."

Dermot wished him good luck in his career and good health to his family. In the circumstances, it was all he could think to say. "Goodbye, Brian," he added.

He watched Murphy turn round, walk back to his car, and drive away, out of his and Alice's life, out of Diseart and its tangled past. He kept the door open, letting out all the shadows that had haunted his dreams. The spectral shapes of the IRA gunmen streamed past him and out into the night.

Alice was asleep in bed, and for a long time he lay beside her, unable to sleep, wondering would the night-time intimidation cease or take on a new guise.

2019

The initial tests confirmed that my mother had suffered a heart attack. The accident and emergency doctors gave her strong doses of medication to stabilise her condition and admitted her to the cardiac ward for further tests and observations. Fortunately, the early results indicated there was little sign of damage to her heart muscle and arteries. Mindful of how busy the ward was and how overworked and harried the nurses looked, my siblings and I organised a nightly rota to keep her company during her stay.

On the first night, I took over from my youngest sister, Edel, at three in the morning. She met me at the ward doors, looking pale and tired. A sign saying no visitors after 8pm hung over the entrance.

"She's been resting since midnight," said Edel.

"Good, she's getting better."

"Not necessarily. We have to wait and see."

The ward looked familiar from my mother's brief stay the previous year. I hoped that this time she would wait for the consultants to carry out all the necessary examinations and not discharge herself too early. My sister showed me the way to her bed, pointing out the curtains around her bed. Then she gave me a quick hug.

"Patricia's coming in at six," she said and slipped away.

Gently, I parted the curtains. My mother appeared to be sleeping, even though she looked uncomfortable, hooked up to monitors and a bag of fluids. Her breathing was soft and easy. When I sat down beside her, she opened her eyes and smiled. Her face looked pale and drawn. She reached out for my hand and urged me to go back home and get a good night's sleep. With any luck, the consultant would let her go home in the morning, she said.

"How are you?" I asked, squeezing her hand.

"I'm feeling fine now. No reason to keep me in with all these old dears."

I smiled and said nothing. When it was clear I was going to stay, she propped herself up on the pillows.

"Listen carefully before I doze off again," she whispered. "There are things I was going to tell you this morning." Suddenly, she looked drawn and vulnerable in her grey nightgown, her face and hair lit up by the bedside lamp.

"You should be resting," I said. "Whatever you want to tell me can wait until you're home."

A shadow fell across her face and her breathing grew laboured. She smiled as if in apology for her condition. "Promise me one thing, make sure you finish your story and get it published."

"I don't think the story will ever be finished. Or published, for that matter."

"But keep writing. If you hit a block, we'll work out a way to finish the story, you and me, in a different way."

I sat for a long time without saying anything. She appeared to doze off but then she opened her eyes and grabbed my hand again.

"Write it in a way that people will believe it," she said. A bright light shone in her eyes. "You must believe in it so much that the readers will believe it, too."

Her eyes closed over, and her breathing settled. Was she forgiving me? Freeing me to write the story I wanted to write? There was barely any sound of her breathing. I thought she was gathering her strength to tell me what I'd wanted to hear for months. She released a long breath, turned her eyes towards me and spoke.

"What else do you want to know about the hijacking?"

But telling me in her current state of health might upset her. I no longer wanted to hear the name of the fourth hijacker. I wanted to talk to her about those bright spring mornings in the 1950s when she was a girl, the sound of the corncrake and the rasp of her father's spade in the potato rig, the geography of field names, places and stories, the ground of Diseart that could be walked upon safely, not the dangerous terrain of the Troubles, the interweave of secrets and silences that were impossible to negotiate.

She took a deep breath. "Go on," she said, "ask me a question."

"Okay, tell me one thing. Why did the IRA speak to you that morning and not dad?"

She smiled and her eyes brightened. "Because I saw them putting on their masks in the hedges. They looked up and saw me watching them. They knew I knew. But they decided to go ahead anyway. That was why they talked to me separately. They wanted me to swear to silence."

And the question I could not ask, I left hanging in the air. My mother had done what was necessary to survive, to raise her family in Diseart. She had wielded her silence like a shield.

"Did you talk about anything else?"

"I tried to persuade them to give up what they were doing. I told them there was still plenty of time to go home and we would never say anything more about it."

"To give up hijacking our car and shooting a policeman?"

"Yes. I had my training as a psychiatric nurse, and I tried to counsel them. What sort of nurse was I if I couldn't make them give up their lunacy?"

"So, you pretended they were patients suffering from some sort of delusion?"

She began to laugh and so did I. "My hands were shaking the whole time," she said. She stopped laughing but her eyes were still bright. "I asked them what good would it do, taking our car and driving off with their guns?" She took a slow breath and gathered her strength. "The leader wanted to talk, but the others didn't. He said it didn't take brave men to come with guns into a house full of children."

I nodded.

"Ask me another question."

"What did you do with the bullet I gave you?"

"I wrapped it in a sweetie wrapper and hid it."

"Why?"

"To make things seem normal."

The gold-coloured bullet was the first thing I thought of when I remembered that morning amid the gamut of greys and shadows, the figures of the IRA men, their masks and guns. It was the one thing that time and memory had preserved clearly.

She told me the story of what she had done with the bullet, and when she had finished, I felt a strange sense of relief. The nightmare that had lived in my imagination, the cold, heartless bullet that had been destined to send my father to an early grave was no longer pointed at him or anyone in my family. Thanks to her words, I no longer felt afraid.

"Any more questions?"

"No. Just rest. You're tired and need your sleep."

My mother closed her eyes and a look of peace fell over her face. I watched her chest expand and contract slowly as she slipped into sleep. Unconscious, her lips began to move, trying to name things that could not be named. I tried to make out the words, but she fell deeper into sleep, and the names were lost.

I listened to the sighs of her breathing and her murmurings. Eventually, I dozed off, too.

I awoke to blue shadowy forms, the nurses floating around in their soft shoes, and the sharp odours of antiseptic and cleaning fluids. The sun had risen. Daylight crept across the shiny hospital floor. There wasn't a sound from my mother. I leaned over and checked her, fearfully, wondering was she still alive. She was deep in sleep, breathing slowly and peacefully.

The silver wheels of the medicine trolley woke her just before six. She looked across at me, as if through a grey veil. Her eyes focused and she reached out to hold my hand.

"You should look for a man called John Harvey," she whispered. "Speak to his aunt, Sadie Brannigan in Ardglushan."

"Who's John Harvey? Another lost relative?"

"Yes. A cousin of mine. His mother is still alive, but it's no good talking to her. She's in a nursing home and hasn't spoken to anyone in years."

I had never heard her mention this side of the family tree before. I marvelled at the complexity of her relations, my relations, how they seemed to keep changing and developing with every story that I was told.

"John Harvey was in our house. That morning." Her voice faded. "He's the last one. The last of the hijackers."

"The last of the hijackers?" At first, I thought I'd misheard. I looked across at her. She reached out and rested her hand lightly on my arm. I thought she was making sure of my company, my listening presence, so that she would not be left alone with the name of the hijacker.

"It was John Harvey who gave you the bullet. The IRA believed he was an informer and he went on the run. There were rumours that he came back, but no one knew for certain what happened to him."

A pair of hands swept back the curtains suddenly, and my sister Patricia entered, laden with fruit and clothes for my mother. For a moment, Patricia's eyes were sharp as needles, watching the two of us, sunk in conspiratorial silence. Then she intervened, dismissing the tense atmosphere with her briskness, stacking fresh fruit and biscuits on her bedside locker. With a sweeping gesture onto the bed, she laid out a new dressing-gown, the corner of which flicked me in the eye. Before she could unleash any more of her gifts upon me, I rose and said my goodbyes. I took a final glance back. My sister was straightening my mother's sheets and asking had the doctor been round yet. The heaviness in my mother's eyes had vanished.

2019

John Harvey.

Now that I had the name in my pocket, and was certain that it was the correct name, I found it unbearable not being able to write more about him. The thought struck me that I had a more important obligation. He'd been involved in murder and should be brought to justice. He should be grilled by the police, not by me, and hauled before the courts. If I were the son of the murdered police officer, and not the guilty bystanders, I'd have gone to the police and demanded his arrest.

I pondered my dilemma as I drove home from the hospital. I only had a name. I didn't know Harvey's whereabouts, or whether he was alive or dead. I had solved the mystery of his identity, but another void opened upon his story. Harvey was guilty of murder, but he might also be guilty of betrayal. But if he was an informer, why had he escaped being shot, the standard punishment for an IRA informer, his body left in a ditch somewhere as a stark warning to other informers? Why were men like Malachy Warde so keen to deny his existence? There must be some other reason to explain why everyone had covered up his identity. Something to do with his character or family history. The kind of man he was and his past. Was it because he was the sort of person from whom everyone could easily disassociate themselves and forget, even my mother, who had been so assiduous in researching her family tree? An odd-man-out. A scapegoat.

I entered the house to the sound of the phone ringing.

Everyone else was still sleeping, so I carefully answered it.

"Hello, again." It was the same parched voice that had called me the previous morning. The same appalling quiet between the words.

"Who is this?" I said.

"You still don't know who I am?" Was there a hint of disappointment in his voice, or exasperation?

"No." I strained to add a face to the voice, but all I could picture was a pair of black lips.

"I gave you a clue. Have you not made any progress?"

I kept my silence and added a pair of eyes, shadowed and glinting, to the voice and lips.

"No? Picture the scene, an old green Renault pulling up at a rundown cottage surrounded by thorn trees. Does that not a ring a bell?" He paused. "I don't think you're giving this your full attention. Okay, let's try another clue. You've written quite a bit about me. Shared my story with others."

As a journalist, I had interviewed and written about a lot of people. Often, I had been too busy writing notes in my jotter to look up and really study the person. A quick handshake, a fleeting look, questions fired at them, and then head-down, the scratching of my pen on paper and then more questions. I'd been too busy concentrating on their words and whatever story I was formulating. A lot of them I probably would not recognise if I met them or heard their voices again. And what of the ones I had used to invent characters in my books in a succession of lurid scenes and crime plots too convoluted to remember without picking up the books and reading them again. All the multitude of people whose stories I had blended together.

"I've written about lots of people."

"But my story was one of the most important you wrote. Here's another clue. I'm the one source of truth hiding behind everything you've written, the one source of light amid all the shadows."

There was only one person he could be talking about.

He must have sensed my thoughts. "Yes, I've been lurking in your imagination for years."

I slammed down the phone. There was no way the caller could be who he was hinting at. Who was he, and what sort of game was he playing? In a flash, I remembered the anonymous calls to our house after the hijacking, my father standing in the hallway with the phone in his hand. Their anonymous persecutors had kept calling, almost every evening, but then one day they had stopped – I was never sure why. Was the caller somehow connected to that time, someone with a secret to hide? I stepped outside into the garden. This was madness. I was winding myself up with old stories of IRA persecution. Who would possibly want to intimidate me into silence, now, after all these years? I sat under the crab apple and hazel trees and stared at the garden where my daughters played on their bikes or read books, swinging in their hammocks. I was sitting in the heart of my parish, surrounded by the echoes of children's laughter and flowing water. Hidden springs shifted beneath me, and the little river that bordered the garden was in full spate. I felt safe here, as in a little ark, surrounded by water and dappled sunlight, a light so comfortable and secure that nothing could go badly wrong under its gentle glow.

The phone rang again. No one ever called me on the landline except complete strangers and my mother. I let it go on.

1982

Alice wasn't in the kitchen or bedroom when Dermot returned home late in the evening. Instead, he found her standing in the living room, watching the final news bulletin of the day, her mouth and eyes wide open.

"Alice?" he said.

She did not answer. He looked at the TV and listened to the newsreader. An undercover SAS squad had struck on a quiet country road in South Tyrone, killing three IRA men in their hijacked van. The footage on the TV news showed an obscenely high number of bullet holes in the vehicle. The photographs of the dead men were the same as the ones in Murphy's folder. He watched the images of sprawled bodies covered with light blue plastic sheets, no longer the young men who had hijacked their car, but dead flesh that needed to be removed from public view.

The newsreader recounted the details of the IRA gang's failed mission to mortar bomb a local army base. He described the reactions of local politicians to the news. But he was secretly saying something else. He was telling the people of Northern Ireland that he had important breaking news for them. Justice, in the context of the Troubles, was something the civilian population no longer understood, something they called justice, but might not be justice after all. Something darker and more dangerous. The security forces had acted as though there were no such things as right and wrong, and the belief in just behaviour and fair treatment of lawbreakers was an encumbrance and ultimately false. But wasn't everyone in the country to blame, too, including him and Alice. They were guilty because of their silence, their worries for their personal safety and that of their family. If they had done things differently, perhaps these young men, their neighbours, and the police officer Ivan White, might have been spared. Once again, Dermot and Alice were the guilty bystanders, the holders of bloody handkerchiefs, and nothing would ever feel the same.

Dermot turned to face Alice. This strange life they had been living since the hijacking, this limbo, should end now, he decided. The woman he had married, Alice Devlin, the young nurse who was an only child, who loved dancing and was devoted to her father, all the hundreds of little things he knew about her, who had been absent since the morning of the hijacking, should now return to him, in body and soul. He didn't believe in ghosts or hauntings, but he wanted the strange shadows to dissolve from her face and disappear forever.

"I'm afraid," she told him.

"Afraid of what? The men are dead. The court case has collapsed. Murphy has closed the investigation."

"I don't know. I just have to forget what I saw."

"Forget what?" Uneasily, his eyes scanned her face.

"What the two of us saw that morning."

"Yes."

But he suspected she was still holding something back. She, too, seemed to take the news of the SAS ambush as a new form of punishment, a warning that they should have rung the police immediately after the IRA gang left with their car and not delayed till after one o'clock, that they should have chosen to raise the alarm as soon as possible, without worrying about the consequences. Dermot thought of the secret powers that had caused the deaths of the young IRA men. He thought of the fourth IRA man and wondered how long it would take before his body turned up in a ditch somewhere. Had he been spared because the security forces still planned to use him? They had killed his comrades. They had killed them to warn him and place him in an impossible position. Dermot wondered were the powers behind the ambush omnipotent and all-seeing. In the pit of his stomach, he almost wished they were.

In that burst of SAS gunfire, a dangerous confrontation had been removed from their lives. Slowly, over the course of weeks and months, they were able to get on with their lives. Murphy never appeared at their door again, and the police didn't seem interested in apprehending the fourth member of the gang. The anonymous phone-calls and the night-time tormentors stopped, too.

No one in the parish talked about the fourth member of the gang. It was as if he had vanished off the face of the earth. Dermot wondered how odd it was that the one member of the gang who survived couldn't be found or didn't want to be found. He assumed there must be someone, in the police force, or among his IRA comrades and relatives, looking for the missing IRA man. There must be something that everyone in the parish, including his wife, wasn't telling him.

A strange, protective silence fell around the fourth member of the gang. It was as if he had disappeared off the face of the earth. The people who knew about his disappearance dared not reveal their knowledge and many people in the parish, who never mentioned his name again, including Alice, became complicit. The months passed by and Dermot found himself a reluctant accomplice to the secret.

For some obscure reason, the silence continued for many years, like a partial eclipse that turns slowly into total darkness; a secret that made neighbours closer than neighbours, relatives closer than relatives, spouses closer than spouses.

2019

A 100 feet high radio tower hung over Sadie Brannigan's little cottage at the side of the mountain in Ballinful. It had been built by the British Army in the early 1990s, not only to help the army and the police broadcast their radio messages, but also to eavesdrop on what was going on in the parish with hi-tech surveillance cameras and listening devices, or so everyone had believed. It had belonged to the general conspiracy of surveillance and secret spying, and fantastical stories had spread about its capabilities.

Even today, long into the ceasefire, something sinister seemed to be brewing around it, gathering amid the whispering grasses and trees. Its forest of radio masts and cameras looked alien and distant, still tuning itself to whatever forces lurked in the parish, the secret powers that ruled the roads and houses.

During the Troubles, the tower had reigned over a realm of silence. The people in its shadow had lived according to the principle of hear nothing, see nothing, say nothing, and men like Malachy Warde had organised the silence, going from door to door, disguised as cheerful farmers or good neighbours, giving out advice or just showing a friendly ear. Vigilance had charged the air, a self-awareness. And the only signs the cameras and listening devices had detected and recorded were unobtrusive ones, a farmer changing his jacket and climbing into his tractor, a car tooting its horn as it passed a certain house, a particular piece of clothing hung on a clothesline, signs that had blended into the fabric of ordinary life, but might have meant something to an invisible watcher, a mission aborted or postponed, or a warning that danger was drawing close.

The sense of surveillance was permanent and universal. I remembered as a teenager how close the military cameras and telescopic lens felt, as though they were constantly on my shoulder, and I might turn round at any moment and mouth some secret message at them. Consciously or not, I felt accused and compelled to blurt out the truth, ready to defend myself by informing on another. But why did I feel guilty? Why the need to exonerate myself? Was it the constant security checkpoints and harassment by soldiers, which felt like a form of punishment and therefore pointed to a hidden crime or violent act that I had done nothing, or not enough to prevent? I was innocent of any wrong-doing but herded in with the guilty.

The woman who answered the door of Brannigan's cottage strongly resembled a teacher who'd taught me at primary school, but then the smell of strong drink hit me, and I saw that it was a different woman with a cloudy confused gaze and a voice not a bit like that of my teacher.

"What do you want?" Her tone was harsh to the point of rudeness.

I apologised for disturbing her and introduced myself as Alice Daly's son, careful to use my mother's maiden name rather than her married one.

"Oh well, if you're Alice's son, I should let you in."

"I won't be long, just a few minutes of your time. We're trying to track down a man called John Harvey and my mother thought you might be able to help."

"Why me?" She leaned forward as if to shut the door in my face but stumbled and grasped onto a handrail.

"He's a lost relative, you might say," I explained.

"A lost relative."

Hesitantly, she led me inside. The hall was a shadowy tunnel that burrowed through boxes of clothes and old magazines. She clicked the light switch, but the bulb had gone, and the place remained in darkness. I looked up and saw cobwebs overlapping cobwebs, and, for a moment, heard a furtive rustling close by. Mice, most likely.

"I haven't seen your mother in years. Ever since I stopped going to Mass."

Through the kitchen window I caught a glimpse of crows wheeling like daredevils in the wind. They made the sombre moor suddenly look like a fun place to be.

"Why are you here?" she asked. She had lost the thread of conversation. Perhaps she had dropped it on purpose. The visit had all the signs of turning out badly, but I persisted. I was going to write about this conversation, and it was my job to derive some meaning or a clue from it. And if there was no meaning or clues here, and I was deluding myself, then that, too, would be worth writing about – my frustration and my foolishness, trying to tell a story that could not be told.

I told her I wanted to find her nephew, John Harvey.

"Why do you want to find him?"

"We're researching the family tree. My mother and John were cousins. There's a missing gap he might be able to fill in."

"My husband Jack used to work with him."

"Would he be able to help us track him down?"

"Jack passed away. A year ago."

"I didn't know that. I'm sorry."

"I think the man you're looking for is dead, too." She licked her lips and avoided saying his name. Even pronouncing the name of a suspected informer had its dangers. "I think the Brits got them all."

"What makes you think that?"

"I get confused thinking about the past. I can't remember who was who and what really happened. So many things took place over a short space of time. I could tell you so many stories and some of them wouldn't be true. But when I think of Harvey, I can remember everything clearly. What happened to him was so unexpected." She sighed and grew silent. Her expression was a blank and I tried to read the expression in her eyes but didn't know how to.

"He vanished one day." She clicked her thumb and forefinger. "Just like that. He drove to the port in Larne, took the ferry to Scotland and was never seen again. His car was left on the ferry, but no body was ever found. His poor mother never got over it. She blamed his former comrades in the IRA for causing his death. There was talk of an informer in the ranks and he was interrogated several times."

As she talked, I tried to map out the chain of events. Of all the things that I learned writing and reading detective novels, the most crucial was that what might appear to be the beginning of the story was not always the first in the sequence of causality. The IRA gang had been killed shortly after the hijacking in 1982, but that did mean the hijacking was the trigger event.

She began talking about the SAS, how they had put on their uniforms and killed people for money. They hadn't cared who they killed, innocent men, women and children. They had carried out their orders and got paid. I asked her another question to get her onto a different track. Instead, she started praising the IRA, telling stories of sacrifice and suffering, the same patriotic stories that had enflamed the emotions of young Irish men and women and swelled the ranks of the IRA.

Listening to her disagreeable voice, saying things I

hadn't heard anyone say in ages, I felt the futility of my situation. I wondered why I was here seeking answers from an eccentric old woman, apart from the excuse that writers and detectives sometimes ask inexplicable questions and travel down dead-ends. My questions were at an end, and I wanted to make a swift escape, drive away and disappear back into the valley. When I got up to say goodbye, she stopped talking and eyed me strangely.

"Which son of Alice's are you. I don't think I've seen you before. She had a son who died. And then there's one who writes poetry.

"That's me. But I write fiction not poetry."

"Someone said you were writing a story about the murder of Tom Donaghy. Is that true?"

"Who told you that?"

"A neighbour of yours. Is it true?"

"I might. I'm not sure yet. Do you know anything about it?"

"I heard my father talk about it many times, but I never listened. Why do you want to write about that?"

Because whenever I mentioned his name, everyone assumed I was talking about his murder, and not the man Donaghy had been, a father and son. It was as if the entire course of his life up until the day of his death had been erased, as if his murderers had swallowed up everything about him and made even his name theirs. And here I was, trying to reverse the situation.

"Because I think there might be a story in it. Somewhere."

Out of the blue, she started talking about the Great Famine, and the things her father had said about the Irish rebellions of the 1800s. "When I was growing up, the old people told stories about the famine as though it were only yesterday," she said. Her eyes grew vague. They seemed to search for another story but then lose its thread. I made to leave.

"Remember, the man you are looking for is dead," she said suddenly.

I nodded. But before I believed her, I would have to see a death certificate.

On my way home, I pulled on to the side of the road at Farrell's hill and stared at the view across the low blue hills of South Tyrone to the Irish Border. A strange feeling preoccupied me. I would have got out for a walk, but the clouds were threatening a sudden downpour. I rolled down the window and listened to the lonely sound of birdcalls. A cold wind funnelled down from the mountain and the sun suddenly emerged from cover. Light filled the moor like the silent flash of a bomb. Bog-pools glittered, and the rain clouds trailed their shadows over leathery hillsides of heather and bracken. I could pinpoint the exact tract of bogland my grandfather had dug turf from as a boy and I had a sudden longing to be out there in the moor, navigating my way past bog trenches, feeling my way along the edges of memory and stories, water gurgling under the peat beds, and the sound of countless droplets cascading down crevices.

About a mile below in the valley, lay the priest's house, a warm-looking bungalow with a pretty garden of rhododendrons, camellias, and trees. But up here, there was no vegetation apart from the thinnest of pine trees and the wiry heather. Perhaps there was no God here either, the houses full of sinners and the bog a realm of darkness trickling violent thoughts into the minds of young men and women. I could see the house belonging to a nursery schoolteacher whose car had been stopped one day by British soldiers and a cache of guns discovered in the boot.

The evening light blazed on the windows of a new two-storey house built by a retired electrician who, in the early 1980s, had detonated a bomb that lay hidden in a culvert. The cottage nearby belonged to a man who had been ostracised by his neighbours because he refused to give shelter to an IRA man on the run. Men and women living under the pressure of a double life. This was the unfinished Ireland of Republicans and diehard paramilitaries, where the sky hung large and low and the land ran all the way to the Irish border, a labyrinth of paths and lanes riddled with bog holes and thorn trees. What on earth had the people here been trying to accomplish?

The horizon darkened and rain began drumming on the roof. The distorted shapes of trees and hills wriggled on the windscreen. I sat in silence. The image of John Harvey in a balaclava rose before me, his eyes bulging, cold and absorbed. In his outstretched hand was the gold-coloured bullet. I could remember him handing me the bullet and whispering, "This is for your daddy if he rings the police before one." No one had ever spoken to me in that way before, with compressed pauses before the words. He had turned round and walked away, heavy-bodied, heavy-booted, with the air of someone just stepping out, leaving the bullet in my safe-keeping, but who would be back very soon for it. He had given me the means of my father's murder. Afterwards, I could never look at my dad in the same light again. For months, I could feel the bullet in my hand, full of Harvey, still belonging to him, heavy and cold. We had an enduring, one-sided connection, initiated by him, forged in the moment he gave me the bullet. It belonged to a darker more violent world, but I was now part of that world. I kept fearing he would sneak back for the bullet, that the leaves and thorns of the blackthorn hedge would rustle and turn into him again. Would my father wake some night to the stomp of his boots and the sight of his loaded gun? Or was the loaded gun this book I was writing? Words could act like bullets, but the words of this story were more like the bullets fired from a gun pointing straight into the sky, injuring no one until their descent back to the ground, striking the shooter and those gathered around him.

My mobile rang. It was Frances. "Where are you now?" she asked.

I hesitated, disorientated, lost in my thoughts. "On the top of Farrell's hill."

"What are you doing there?" There was a hint of reproach in her voice.

"Thinking."

"It's Tuesday evening. The girls have their music lesson at six."

"I'm coming back now."

"Okay. Did you find out anything interesting?"

"Possibly. I think Harvey is either dead or he staged his own disappearance. He might be living somewhere under a false name."

"If he changed his name by deed poll, there'll be an official record of it somewhere."

"I don't think a former IRA man would do it that way."

"Then that will make it impossible to find him."

"I thought so, too. But people who try to hide from the past always end up making some connection with their old life. There must be someone, somewhere who knows where he is or what he is doing."

I drove home at speed.

First thing the next morning, the phone rang.

"Worked out who I am yet?" said the dry voice.

"No."

"I don't think you're taking this game too seriously. Here's my final clue. You discharged me from my duties three years ago."

"Discharged you?"

There was a defiant silence from his end of the phone.

"When you finished the last of your detective series. That's right, it's Inspector Celcius Daly here at your service."

Clearly, my mysterious caller was a joker.

"You haven't always made things easy for me, but I'm not going to hold that against you."

I gave a sharp laugh.

"You know the best scenes in your books are when it's just me and the landscape."

Daly was so alive in my imagination that for a moment I almost believed my mysterious caller. Whoever he was, I was impressed he had read enough of my books to work out their central flaw.

"That's your opinion." But he was right. "It's easier to imagine landscapes than write about the events of the Troubles."

"But even the Troubles should be told through the imagination."

Who was he, another writer needling me with doubts?

"And without fear," he added. "I've read your account of the IRA hijacking in a couple of your books, and I've come to a conclusion. You didn't understand a single thing even though you were right there in the living room. You must have buried your head in a book or looked out the window the whole time the IRA gang were there."

I froze with silence.

"Not a single thing, son." He was quiet for so long that I thought the line had gone dead. When he spoke again, he

Anthony J. Quinn

lowered his voice. "The IRA man who gave you the bullet. He wasn't killed in the SAS ambush, you know that, don't you? He disappeared without a trace."

"Who told you that?"

"That's for you to find out. I know a lot more than you think."

A sound behind me made me turn round. My eldest daughter was standing in the hallway, watching me with unblinking eyes. What did she make of this strange conversation, her father talking and listening to the whispering secrets of his fictional detective? I ushered her into the kitchen and indicated that she should get the cereal bowls out.

"Time is running out," said the voice. "Soon all the secrets will be taken to the grave."

"You don't know what you're talking about," I said in an attempt to goad him into saying more.

"I know exactly what I'm talking about."

"But how can you?"

"Believe me, I do."

"What else do you know about the hijacking?"

"It was a very murky time."

"Too murky to ever find out the truth."

"I didn't say that. I just don't want you to get your hopes up."

"Look, I know you're someone connected to the hijacking."

"Who exactly do you think I am?" It was his turn to goad me.

"I think you're the fourth member of the IRA gang. I think you're John Harvey." I had always believed that I would recognise Harvey's voice at once. One word would have been sufficient, even if he had aged or his voice had been deformed by illness. I'd have recognised it instantly.

184

But I wasn't sure if this was the same voice I'd heard that morning in 1982.

"Who told you that name?"

"It doesn't matter who told me. I know you were in my house on the morning of the hijacking. It was you who gave me the bullet."

"Did you find out anything else about this John Harvey?"

"What else is there to find out?"

"Nothing much. But I suggest you go and search his home place. The cottage where he lived with his mother. I'll ring again tomorrow, and you can tell me what you find there."

I put the phone down and walked into the kitchen where Frances and my daughters were having breakfast.

"Who was that? Your mother?"

"No," I answered vaguely. "Just something to do with a story."

Anthony J. Quinn

2019

Harvey's homeplace lay completely immersed in the shadow of a mountain, a row of pine trees forming a high rampart against the wind and sun, the same fixed view of tree trunks and densely needled branches that had travelled alongside me for miles on the single-track road. I felt a physical sensation, a tightness in my throat, as I stared at the strange depths within the trees.

An air of dereliction hung around the cottage, its front turned discreetly away from the road, its windows either broken or blank and empty. The walls on the north side were green with moss, and weeds had crept through the guttering, poking their heads along the line of the roof. The Sperrin Mountains were full of decomposing cottages like these, tucked away amid the gloom of gorse and thorn thickets. A cold breeze wafted down from the mountain top and the pine trees should have been moving, but they were completely still, adding to the eerie mood of the place. I checked the back door and saw that it had been splintered open with a crowbar. At some point in the past, an intruder had made a forced entry. Whatever the fate of John Harvey, his cottage had been unable to keep the violent world at bay.

I stumbled through the cottage's cramped rooms. In the kitchen, I found a pile of empty Guinness bottles in a cupboard, a faded holy calendar and a small table, showered with bird droppings and twigs. There were frayed carpets throughout, worn by restless feet, and a sleeping bag unrolled on a rotten mattress in one of the bedrooms. The strong odour of decay filled the air. Yet the house was not completely empty. I could feel something lurking within, a message, waiting for its hour, hiding beneath the curling wallpaper, in the cracked upholstery, in the patterns of mildewed damp decorating the walls. I kept searching, but the only sign of life was a rat I uncovered in the bathroom. It stared at me in dumb silence before scuttling away. I stepped outside and gazed at the backdrop of pine trees, the strip of bogland and brown heather interleaved with black trenches, everything perfectly still and detached, as though the entire mountain side were dead and hostile to the gaze of the living. The sun disappeared behind a ridge and the shadows exaggerated the steepness of the mountain. I looked up where the last of the evening light shone on the heather and bracken.

A sudden urge to return home to my desk filled me. I preferred the clean whiteness of an empty page, the closeness of words when reading and writing, the sense of a living testimony, a secret message when sentences are completed, and even dead landscapes are endowed with meaning. There was nothing else for me to do but sit down and write the story, and this I should do immediately, while it was still fresh in my mind. I would end the book with a chapter describing the various rumours about Harvey's whereabouts and his possible demise, finish the story without drawing any conclusions or offering any opinions. Visiting Harvey's house would be the final scene, and my mother would be relieved, and so would my neighbours at not hearing Harvey's name mentioned again. I'd clear my desk of all the notes and get back to writing fictional detective stories.

But ending it that way felt like a clerical chore. I would be leaving it to someone else to read between the lines and pick out the grain of truth from the overwhelming chaff. If only I could meet Harvey, talk to him and listen to his story, and form some sort of connection. I might understand why his neighbours and the IRA had taken that drastic step, from trusting him within their ranks to denying his existence altogether.

I was about to turn back to my car when I saw a red Land Rover jeep flash through the trees. Its garish colour seemed at odds with the ruin of the house. The jeep pulled up alongside my car, and the figure of a man emerged. His face was familiar, sharp and cunning, like a wild animal's, searching for and registering the location of its prey. The green eyes of Malachy Warde fixed upon me.

"Well, is this the end of your story?" he said jovially.

"What story is that?"

"The one about the man who lived here."

"Almost," I said, surveying the derelict house.

"Good, that's all I wanted to know." He turned and kicked at the rusted heap of a wheelbarrow. "What a dump."

I stared at him. This might have been the final page if he hadn't turned up. But now that he had, the story felt even more like an unfinished work, a search for a missing man that had barely begun.

"Wait," I said. "Do you know where John Harvey is?"

"Me?"

"Yes."

"Haven't a clue. Like everyone else in the parish."

"Do you think it's right no one talks about him? It's as if he never existed."

I watched his stare intensify. I had overstepped the mark. But I pushed on.

"Is it because he was an informer?"

Warde shrugged. "There were rumours, but I can't talk about them."

"Who told you not to?"

He didn't reply.

"Was he killed by the IRA?"

He didn't react as I expected. He didn't react at all. His gaze fell on me, aloof and silent. We were on the dark side of the mountain and Harvey belonged to the dark side of memory. If he had been murdered, the news of his death had never been allowed to reach the living. It belonged to somewhere beyond the limits of the parish. And if he hadn't been killed then he'd vanished as people did in old stories and fairy-tales, spirited away by an evil wind or a sneaking mist brewed up by the murky atmosphere of the Troubles. Yet, there was something steadfastly true about the dilapidated home - the irrefutable signs that he and his mother had once lived in this place, before someone had taken him away. His disappearance was beyond understanding, but also beyond doubt.

"You don't know for sure if he's dead or not," I said. "That's what you're telling me, isn't it?"

There was a long moment of silence and then Warde spoke in a low voice. "I'm not allowed to tell you about Harvey. You'll have to go to someone higher up."

"Who?"

"I could arrange a meeting for you with the right man." He took out his mobile phone.

"Okay," I said, somewhat thrown by his sudden offer of help.

He walked off and began mumbling into his phone. After making several phone calls, he walked back to me.

"He's happy to speak to you," he said, flashing me a slightly condescending look. "Are you free to come right now?"

My first instinct was to decline the invitation. Things were progressing too quickly.

"Come on, I've had to twist his arm. He's a busy man and you might not get the chance to talk to him again. He asked me to drive you over to his local pub."

"Just the three of us?"

"Yes, you, me and the head honcho himself. He doesn't like having lots of people around."

"Okay."

A grin spread across his face. "Don't bother pestering him with questions. If he wants to tell you what happened to Harvey, he will. If he doesn't, there's no point asking."

"Did you tell him why I want to know?"

"I told him you were working on a book." Warde's grin increased. "He sounded interested."

I climbed into his jeep and fifteen minutes later we pulled up at a country pub in Rossclean. Cars were pulled up in the small car park, and a group of young men stood outside, talking to each other. They turned and nodded to Warde. Inside, the elderly men at the bar wore looks of benign mistrust when they saw us enter, as though Warde had broken an unspoken rule by bringing a stranger here, one which they were prepared to overlook for the time being.

2019

Harvey led me up a set of back stairs to a darkened attic room and guided me to a chair. The only sound was that of crows scrabbling along the rooftop and the flap of their wings. And then someone coughed. "Come a little closer, I want to see you," said a voice. My eyes, adjusting to the lack of light, made out the silhouetted shape of a thick-set man facing me at a low desk. Suddenly I felt like a hapless journalist who had stumbled into a dangerous warzone and hadn't the wit to escape.

However, in spite of the setting, my host was less taciturn than I expected. He was reserved, but when he greeted me by my Christian name, I was surprised by his friendly tone, as though he were genuinely glad I had come to ask him questions about Harvey. Perhaps Warde had been lying when he told me he'd had to twist arms to arrange the meeting. Then it struck me that Warde, or even the local bigwigs in the IRA might have proposed the idea of the meeting themselves and organised it in advance – time to pull that reporter fella in and learn something about the book he's writing. In all likelihood, they had been planning the meeting since I'd first asked Warde about the fourth hijacker. If this were the case, what sort of trap had I stepped into? The security arrangements, the darkened room and the neutral venue also suggested a measure of pre-planning. More warning signs.

"John Harvey," said the silhouette with a sigh. "For a long time, I was sick of hearing that man's name. What have you heard about him?"

I kept it as bland as possible and recounted the few

facts I knew. "He was a member of a renowned IRA brigade, yet no one speaks of him. He vanished without trace and I keep asking myself why…"

I trailed off and the silhouette seemed to harden into a statue.

"Are you asking yourself or are you asking me?"

I hesitated. "Well now that you put it that way, yes, I am asking you."

Warde had been standing at the door, but now the silhouette swept his hand and signalled him to leave.

"Nothing I say can be quoted in a newspaper," he said, shifting position. I caught a glimpse of a crew-cut head, peppered with silver.

"Of course. I just want to know if Harvey is still alive."

"Who's to say if he's alive or not. There are many forms of death. Ever since the ceasefire, I've felt half-dead myself. Harvey might be living under a new identity and the old John Harvey we all suspected was collaborating with the enemies of Ireland is long dead."

"What sort of man was he?"

"He was a daredevil and a fool, and he always hungered for self-worth." There was a tiredness in his voice, a tiredness made up of decades of brutal secrets. "He enjoyed the status of being in the IRA, but his big weakness was gambling. He was hooked on horse-racing and had a desperate need for cash to fuel his addiction. He must have been an easy target for Special Branch and the RUC's intelligence war. If an informer came clean and admitted to us that they'd been turned it would be alright. But we would kick them out of the IRA, and Harvey could never have faced that."

"But his friends, his neighbours, his family, were all Republicans and IRA supporters. How could he have betrayed them to the police?"

"I've seen it before in informers. They're happy to sit like spiders at the centre of a web of lies. Harvey liked being the focus of attention. Made him feel important. I could see it in him. Well, he got what he wanted."

"But so much so that he risked getting shot?"

He sighed. "Call it a death-wish if you want. When Harvey was told about the mounting suspicions hanging over him, he said nothing and just gave a little sideways smile. I was there on both occasions. He was due to come back for a third occasion, but he scarpered."

For a moment, I thought I could understand the loneliness Harvey must have felt. The safest thing to do would have been to put as much distance as possible between himself and his IRA comrades. "How strong was the evidence against him?" I asked.

"Strong, but not strong enough to be sufficient. On the other hand, manys a man was found guilty on weaker grounds."

"And shot?"

He paused. "After his second interrogation, he took the car ferry to Scotland but never got off the boat, at least that was how it seemed."

"What do you mean?"

"His car was left on the vehicle deck. He never drove it off the ferry. An old blue Datsun with a suitcase of his clothes in the boot."

I thought I could remember meeting the same car, jolting over the bog roads of Diseart under wide blue skies or heavy rain, snaking amid the hedges or swerving into blind corners. The cars of so many young men were always speeding on the parish roads, going nowhere and everywhere.

"At first, his poor mother thought he'd abandoned the

car and just walked off the ferry, but weeks and months went by with no news about him. People started coming up with all sorts of explanations for what had happened."

"Like he might have fallen overboard or committed suicide?"

"Worse than that."

It grew cold in the room, or perhaps his words made me feel cold. I stared at the dim outline of table and chairs, drawing relief from the familiar domestic objects.

"A story went round that he'd been killed and stuffed in the boot of a car and then buried somewhere in the Scottish Lowlands. All I can tell is the killing wasn't sanctioned by me or anyone from the South Tyrone brigade of the IRA. We were more like an extended family than a military hierarchy. If we had found him guilty, we would have made sure his body went back to his family."

Crossing the sea with a dead body in the boot sounded a bit much, even for a bloodthirsty wing of the IRA. But they might well have dumped his body overboard under cover of darkness.

"If Harvey didn't betray the other IRA men, then someone else must have."

"That's possible." He was silent for a while. "That's everything I can tell you about Harvey. If you don't like it, make up your own story. That's what writers do, isn't it?" He turned to one side, and I saw his eyes, glinting with an unstable light.

"Just one more question. Did you think he was an informer, or did you believe he was innocent?"

The silhouette cursed and shook his head. "Harvey was guilty. I'm sure of that, but I'm not sure exactly what he was guilty of. He was a mystery to all who knew him. You could spend months talking to everyone who knew him and still know nothing about him. We had all sorts in our ranks, especially after the British started arresting everyone and interned half the country, but I never came across anyone quite like Harvey." He stopped. His exasperation had goaded him into saying more than he intended.

"So that was it, you let him go free?"

But I was talking to myself. The silhouetted head had shifted. The door opened and Warde stood framed in the light. I turned sharply. My neck had grown stiff with stillness and the tension of the interview.

"Take him back to the car," said the silhouette. "I need some fucking air."

I had blundered into something bigger, something I could not understand nor wish to. I got into the front passenger seat and Warde slammed the door shut on me. Then he climbed into the driver seat. It had grown dark outside. The lights of houses shivered in the valley. The car sped through the back roads, hitting potholes and culverts, the thump, thump noise reminding me of the bodies of informers bundled up in the boots of cars and driven by men like Warde. When he returned me to my car at Harvey's abandoned home, he made an effort to be friendly again. He even smiled as I stepped out of his car.

"I've something for you to think about," he said. "Have you considered what the alternative theory might be?"

I hesitated.

"Who else could have betrayed the IRA gang? Suppose it wasn't Harvey. Who else could it be? Who else knew beyond any doubt who hijacked your car that morning?" He gave a little wave. "Don't forget to tell your mother I was asking for her."

The next morning, I awoke to the sound of the phone ringing. Stumbling, slightly out of breath, half-running down the stairs I made it to the phone before anyone else did.

"Detective Celcius Daly here. Before you put down the phone, a word of warning. If you want to find out the truth about John Harvey don't cut me off again."

"Who are you? What do you want from me?"

"I've been playing games with you for too long. It's time we had a meeting. Face-to-face." He gave me the name of a coffee shop in Armagh City and a time, one pm. And then the line went dead.

My meeting with the caller could not be postponed. If I didn't turn up, he would call again and torment me with more clues. A circle of faces and names spun around me: John Harvey, Malachy Warde, the dead IRA men, as though I were on a carousel, revolving too quickly to make stepping off a safe move. I would have to hold on and wait for it to stop at one face, one name.

2019

The man who rose to shake my hand was vaguely familiar, in his early seventies, and excessively thin. I could see the unease in his eyes as soon as I entered the upstairs room in the coffee shop, and he looked up at me. The feeling of apprehension was mutual.

An instant after I glimpsed it, the anxious look disappeared from his eyes. He coughed self-consciously, introduced himself as Brian Murphy and shook my hand with the formal courtesy of a retired police detective. We stared at each other for several moments, and then he spoke.

"For a moment there, I thought you were your father. How is he these days?"

"So, the caller was you?"

He nodded.

I needed time to think this through properly. My coffee arrived and I drank it with a gulp.

"Your friend, the chief inspector, told me you were researching the hijacking," he explained. "And then you rang and left your number. I decided I had to do something."

"Why?"

He smiled weakly. "I had no clear plan. Even when I was making the phone calls, I asked myself what I was really hoping to gain. Ever since retiring, I've been thinking over things. Going through unsolved cases. In those days, there were all sorts of grudges and rivalries between the security services."

"But that doesn't answer my question."

"What question?"

"Why did you pretend to be Celcius Daly?"

"After you left your message, I checked you out on the internet and saw that you'd written these books about a Catholic police detective. I read the reviews from the newspapers, and the interviews, and I thought good for you. Then I picked up a couple of your books in the library. I was intrigued by your detective. He drove the same car I drove back in those days, a green Renault, was separated and lived on his father's farm. The more I read, the more intrigued I got. There's something about seeing yourself in a fictional character and reading about the types of cases you once investigated yourself. And then I thought this fictional character might be good for me, too. So, I rang you and introduced myself as Inspector Daly."

Now I understood the tone of self-mockery I had heard in his voice. The reference to Daly had been a joke at his own expense. During those dark months in 1982, Murphy had been a compelling figure, well-dressed, but a little rough looking, visiting our home in the evenings and talking to my father on the porch or in the kitchen, the embodiment of a dogged kind of detective confidence that I had resurrected in Celcius Daly. Murphy had opened doors in my boyhood imagination, the questions he had asked, his lurking presence, his conflicted identity as a Catholic officer in a predominantly Protestant police force. He had been the inspiration for Daly, no doubt about it.

"I didn't mean to deceive you," he said. "I just wanted to find a way to guide you in the right direction without compromising myself."

But he was a retired police detective. He didn't need to pretend to be anyone else. "You did deceive me. That's the point. You made up a character and pretended to be him."

"No, you're the one who made up Celcius Daly, not me," he said quietly. "You took what you remembered of me, the car I drove, my family circumstances, even the type of house I was living in and created this morose detective who helped you sell some books. You've rewritten my story and the story of the Troubles to fit in with your crime fiction plots."

But I had only been trying to forge a career as a writer. There was nothing wrong with that, was there? I hadn't meant to mix up the truth with lies, at least not at the start.

Murphy leaned back and sized me up. "You were the eldest son, the one who was given the bullet?"

"Yes."

"You were all so small back then and looked the same."

He looked at me some more. "Well, now that we've been properly introduced, what do you want to know?"

"Your memories of those months in 1982."

Murphy was not keen on speaking about himself or his role as a police detective, only about the situation my parents found themselves in. Several times, he expressed sympathy for the difficult decisions they had faced, but he appeared to have tossed aside any concerns about the pressure he had placed them under, all the unspoken encouragements and threats. As the investigating detective, he talked about what he wanted to talk about, nothing else. It was clear the legal and procedural facts of those stressful six months were his mental property and no one else's.

He stared at me with a slight smile. "I was told to arrest your father, if necessary, and bring him in for questioning. But I decided against that. I talked to him like I was an old friend. I wanted to win over his confidence." The smile turned into a grimace. "Your parents were lucky they got me and not some hot-headed bastard with loyalist connections."

"Yes. They were fortunate."

"And I was good to them. Never pushed them too far."

"My father always said he was glad you were the investigating detective. Surprised but glad."

"Why do you want to know more about Harvey?"

"He was the one who gave me the bullet. I want to look him in the eye again. He made me part of the story, and, in a way, neither of us can escape its telling."

He looked at me oddly, as well he might. My explanation was directed not just at him but at an invisible group of people neither of us had met, the future readers of my book.

"There's no way to prove he was in your house that morning."

"I'm not looking for proof. I just wanted to find out what happened to him and why the mystery. Every time I mention his name, I feel I'm talking into a void."

More than anything else, I wanted to hear Harvey's story and an explanation for his behaviour, all the events and betrayals that had occurred through him and around him, the unexpected turn of events, and what had driven him towards the strange life he had led.

"Why were my father's details leaked to the IRA's solicitor?" I asked.

"It was a procedural error. I told your parents as much. Are you looking for some other explanation?"

"Can you give me one?"

"No."

"It's an important question. For my parents and me."

"You want something sinister for your book. You want me to say it was to distract attention from an informer, someone like Harvey."

"Something like that."

"It was not like that at all." He sighed. "I was the lead detective in the case, but other forces were in control. After the SAS ambush, Special Branch closed the case." He glanced at me. "But the case was never properly closed."

"What did Special Branch know?"

He gave a derisive snort. "Special Branch never discussed anything."

"But they were involved?"

"I gave my reports to my commander, and he did whatever he had to do with them. I suppose he must have passed them over to Special Branch. Those boys were always tight-lipped."

What he was saying was true. I had heard from other RUC detectives that Special Branch had jealously guarded its information, especially when it came to informers.

"Let me give you an example. They gave us fingerprints to compare with the ones we took from recovered weapons, hijacked cars, all the forensic scenes we investigated. But the fingerprints never had any names, only numbers. We had to compare them blind. When I asked my commander why we were doing blind comparisons for Special Branch he said don't ask. Everything was passed to him. And he handed it over to Special Branch. We never knew if there were any hits or not."

"Did Harvey work for Special Branch? Was he their informer?"

Murphy sighed again. "There were so many informers and intelligence units back then. Operations hidden within operations. The system was run on a need-to-know basis, otherwise the entire network would have collapsed."

"I just want to know about Harvey."

He looked around nervously and leaned back, trying to play the part of a respectable retiree enjoying his afternoon coffee. "Back then I kept my head down and watched my back. It was a violent, treacherous little country we were policing." A grimace tugged at his lips. "Still is."

Why was he being so evasive? Was it to protect Harvey's reputation or his own?

"Has someone instructed you not to talk about Harvey?" I asked. "Is this still confidential?"

Murphy stared at me. "I've been retired for almost twenty years. I've received no instructions from my superiors about what I can or cannot say about the investigations I carried out." He leaned forward again, with the air of a man eager to show that he had nothing to hide. "One thing I know for certain about Harvey was that he didn't die on that ferry. He left behind his car and suitcase, walked off as a foot passenger and started a new life in Scotland."

"How do you know that?"

"Harvey had to keep in touch with Special Branch. To organise his payments."

So, it was true, Harvey was a paid informer.

"Rather than receiving a lump sum, which is what Special Branch normally gave their operatives, Harvey insisted upon a monthly payment sent to his new address in Scotland. The payments were spread over 16 years."

"Which meant they ended in 1998."

"Correct."

I was surprised and disappointed. If the cheques had been cashed then Harvey had been alive for much longer than anyone in the parish believed, but the most recent address would have been more than twenty years old. Would the trail have run cold by now?

"Harvey kept on the move in Scotland. He reported

numerous changes of address. He never really settled down. Sometime in 1986, he reported his final change of address to his handlers. The cheques were redirected to his mother's address. For the last twelve years they were cashed each month by his mother."

"Why do you think he did that?"

"He had moved back. To Diseart. He was living with his mother in secret."

"But why? Surely he was risking his life?" I stared at him blankly.

"Informers are interesting and complex characters. In spite of all their cunning, they sometimes do the stupidest things. Instead of lying low after he had faked his own death on the ferry and taking his chances with a new name in Scotland, Harvey went back home with the intention of living right under the eyes and noses of the people he betrayed."

"But why?"

"He missed his home and his tightly knit family. He lacked the social skills and confidence to start a new life in a strange environment. About a week after he staged his disappearance, he phoned his mother and told her what he had done. He phoned her every day afterwards. He grew up in a cocooned world and he missed it badly."

The more I thought about what Murphy was telling me, the more I realised there was no longer a mystery to his character. Harvey had been like any other son of Diseart, carrying the gravitational pull of home wherever he went. I understood how great the draw had been for Harvey. His attachment to his home and his mother had brought him back. But he had lived the life of a shadow, hiding under his mother's protection, and she had guarded his game of hide and seek, guarding not her son, but his future, nursing him back to some form of life as the country underwent the tectonic shifts of the IRA ceasefire, the Good Friday Agreement and a new millennium.

In fact, in some senses, Harvey was almost my double. I felt a slight sense of fear and revulsion at the thought. Harvey's fate had revealed a flaw that filled me with a helpless sadness. At certain points in our lives, when we could have broken away, we had suffered from a similar lack of courage.

"A nice little twist, don't you think?" said Murphy.

I had to admit that it was intriguing. And it painted Harvey in a much more sympathetic light, unable to find his bearings in the world, compelled to return home and face the danger of an informer's death.

"Is Harvey still alive? Do you know his whereabouts?"

"There's only one person who can tell you exactly what happened to John Harvey."

"Who?"

"His mother."

"But she lives in a nursing home and is unable to speak."

"Can't speak or won't speak?" Murphy reached round to grab his coat. "Tell her you know that Harvey came back from Scotland and was living with her in secret up until the early 2000s. Watch her reaction."

I got up to leave. "One more thing before I go. If the information about my father's evidence wasn't leaked to protect Harvey, was it to protect someone else, a more important source of information?"

He looked at me with a glint of curiosity. "No. Why do you ask?"

"Just a thought I had. It would fit a pattern."

He lifted his mobile phone from the table and began turning it over and over. "You're digging in all directions."

"Trying to find a tunnel towards the light."

He stared at me with an expression that was not exactly hostile or worried. "It's always good to find the light."

"My aim is to describe everyone's role in what happened."

He looked thoughtful. "Just make sure you do justice to the truth," he said.

I blinked. "As much as is possible." What he had said had somehow unnerved me. "I have to remember to tell all sides of the story."

He was cool and polite, again. "Be careful. No matter how hard you try to be fair, whatever you write will always be too much. You're going to tilt the balance one way or the other. Do you understand what I mean?"

I nodded without really answering. I reached over and shook his hand. Was that a knowing smirk or the trace of an encouraging smile on his face?

"The most important thing I learned in the RUC," he said, "was once something's done, it can never be undone. There's always a price to pay."

I left, preoccupied by his parting words. They had the ring of truth. There always was a penalty.

2019

The next morning it was raining heavily, and I rose with a feeling that I was suffocating. I looked through the bedroom window at the drenched, murky trees and thought people like Harvey and I would never escape. We were prisoners of this parish and its dark roads, unable to fit in anywhere else, and the rain would eventually drown us.

I went outside and breathed the leaf-purified air. The rain stopped and everywhere around me I could feel the softness of the landscape, like cotton wool, closing in and smothering everything, the little glen full of trees and cushioned with shadows, the church on the hill and its graveyard, landmarks of a deadly stillness. However, I no longer felt distressed or fearful. I told myself that I had returned to this parish of my own will and was not part of its silence.

I got into the car and drove. I wanted to free something inside me, something twisted and cramped, the ghost of Harvey trapped within my body, the informer in my soul, who would never be at ease living in this kingdom of secrets.

Unanswered questions hung before me as I entered the double doors of the nursing home. The nurse manager met me at the reception and walked me through a long corridor past an inner courtyard. As it happened, she knew my mother very well and was fond of her. They met up regularly and liked to entertain each other with stories of their student nursing days and the Civil Rights marches they had joined in the late 1960s. I told her about my mother's recent heart attack, and she promised to visit her soon.

"I'd like to see your mother talking to Mary Harvey," she said. "She'd know the right questions to ask and get the stories out of her."

Perhaps that was it. No one had asked her the right questions before. Who knew, perhaps she had been waiting all these years for someone to come and ask them?

The manager explained how the residents in the nursing home fell into two distinct groups, even those with dementia or who were severely incapacitated by strokes. The first group refused to mention the past. Perhaps they had repressed their memories or forgotten them entirely. The second group saw it as their duty to remember and talk about the past. They didn't want to forget, and they didn't want others to forget either.

"They sit with their backs to those who don't talk," she said. "They make use of their memories to pass the time and amuse each other. They like to gossip. They aren't afraid to ask questions and are trustful enough to answer them. I'd say there's not a single tiny corner of their lives they haven't shared over and over again."

I thanked her for her time. I had no doubt which group Mary Harvey belonged to.

A Polish care assistant was hoovering the sunroom when I entered. I asked for Mary Harvey and she seemed surprised. Some of the residents were sleeping; the others sat motionlessly and peered at me with curiosity.

"Poor Mary, no one has visited her in years," said the care assistant, pointing to an elderly woman sitting in a corner. Mary Harvey's hair was combed and neat as a doll's. Her head leaned slightly to one side, propped on a soft white pillow, and her calm eyes stared out through the window. In her gaze, I thought I detected a hint of defiance.

The room was very warm, and the palms of my hands prickled with sweat. An untouched cup of tea and a buttered scone sat at Mary's side table. There were crumbs on her blouse and her eyes turned towards me and then back at the empty window. Even the flowers on the windowsill seemed to be sleeping, their petals folded up and drooping in the warmth. I felt uncomfortable sitting down beside her. Those who were awake held me with a mute stare. Mothers, grandmothers, sisters, aunts, as aloof from the outside world as statues.

"I'm sorry to bother you," I said. "My mother's Alice Devlin. I'm writing a story and I'd like to find out what happened to your son, John."

She sank a little deeper into her chair. Had I put the question too bluntly? She began breathing harder. I was aware of the woman beside her watching me intently. Her hair was more dishevelled than Mary's and the armrests of her armchair grubbier. When I glanced at her, she looked away. There was something crafty about her expression. I grew apprehensive, aware of the room full of motionless witnesses. I had hoped to talk to John's mother somewhere more discreet.

I made my request again and waited. At the start, she paid little attention to me and seemed unused to having anyone talk directly to her. Strangely, however, she did not avoid my gaze. When I looked at her, she held my stare, openly and without apprehension, and then glanced away as though the subject had been thoroughly discussed already and there were no longer any secrets to probe.

"I know it's a difficult thing to talk about," I said to Mary. "Can you hear me?"

"Yes, I can hear you," she replied.

I apologised again and said I was anxious to find out what had happened to her son. I waited, determined to let her talk since any more explaining might put her off.

"Who did you say you were?"

"Alice Devlin's son."

The care assistant poured me a milky cup of tea from the trolley and then rolled it out of the room.

"What do you want?" Mary raised her chin and gave me a stare, half disdainful, half troubled, as though my presence was something she would have to suffer. I wanted to tell her that her son had handed me a bullet when I was eleven years old to buy my father's silence. Our paths had crossed more than thirty years before. He had probably forgotten me and my name and done other things with bullets to people whose names and faces he'd also forgotten. But the memory had stayed with me.

"I want to find out what happened to your son, John."

I waited and searched her face for any signs she had understood my question. Amid the tired wrinkles of her face, her eyes seemed full of sadness. I could hear her breath, rasping and uneven. The room was so silent, and her breathing stood out with disturbing clarity. What was the point of bothering her? She had not spoken of her son for years. I rose to leave, but then her chair creaked, and she leaned forward slightly. Her hand groped towards me. If she was still breathing, there was no sign of it. She gathered her strength and released a long sigh.

"Sit," she said.

I lowered myself into the seat.

"You remind me. Of him."

"John was involved in the Troubles, and I'd like to tell his story. Future generations won't appreciate the decisions young men like him had to make."

She didn't respond. Her breathing slowed. Then she

leaned towards me and whispered. "I'll tell you about John another day." She reached out and squeezed my arm. I glanced round and realised the eyes of the other residents were fixed upon us. They were all awake now, frozen in different positions of rapt attention, as though a cold wind had suddenly passed through the room and shook them from their rest. Why was I here, bothering an elderly woman who had experienced enough heartbreak in her life? I desperately wanted to find out what had happened to Harvey so that I could...do what exactly? Finish the book and understand more about my parish and ultimately myself? Or was it all just a writer's whim. I looked at the old woman beside Mary. Her gaze was fixed stubbornly upon me, watchful yet evasive. Silence filled the air. Finally, I took the plunge.

"I'd like to hear about John, now," I said trying to keep the urgency out of my voice, but there was no mistaking the forceful tone.

Mary's eyes sharpened. "I haven't seen him in years," she replied.

"I heard that he came back from Scotland and lived with you. He didn't die on the ferry. He got off as a foot passenger and started a new life in Scotland. Later he moved back to Diseart. The rest of the world thought he was dead, but he was right under your nose."

She snorted. "Who told you that?"

"Someone who knew his plans."

"What else did they tell you?"

"That he was a good son, devoted to you."

"A good son? Dear me." She frowned but a sadness took hold in her eyes. "He was devoted to more things than me. He got himself into bad trouble."

"Who else knew he was living with you?"

"No one."

"Are you sure?"

Her eyes watered slightly. "Yes...there was someone else, but I trusted him. He never said a word about it to anyone."

"Who?"

"A priest."

"Was there anyone else? Did he have any friends? Anyone I can speak to who could tell me more."

"Friends? John was a loner."

"But a good son."

"He never wanted to leave me. Does that mean he was a good son?"

I sipped the tea and waited, but she fell back into silence.

"I need to ask you an important question, Mrs Harvey. Are you waiting for him? Might he come here some day and visit you, or send someone as a messenger?"

She shook her head, slowly, pointedly. "John is waiting for me. One day soon I'll meet him."

Time passed. The silence in the room felt hollow, mixed with the rasping sighs of the old women and the dry clicks of the clock on the wall. My tea went cold. I understood that Mary would tell me nothing more. I looked around and saw that the eyes of the others were fixed upon me. The heat in the room grew stifling, the gaze of the old women oppressive. Rain fell and the light in the room softened, but still their gaze did not relax, watching me intently, poking me with their silent mistrust. A room filled with muteness, its residents sitting on guard. The secrecy of people like Malachy Warde and his IRA commander was less powerful than the severity of their silent vigilance.

Harvey had lived by the code of his times. A man who had done violent things but whose aggression had been lost in the scale of violence carried out during the Troubles, a minor figure who had betrayed his comrades like so many others, who had handed me a bullet with a dark promise and then faded into the general background of threats and betrayals of those grim decades. The true horror of his fate was that his ghost now lay in this room, trapped in a twilight space, half-forgotten, half-remembered, and it would be impossible to discover anything more about his disappearance or learn anything morally from his mysterious fate.

I had no more questions to ask. I had bothered Mary Harvey enough. I had wanted her to have the final word. She was one of the last people to see him alive, and it was fitting that the story should end here, with her silence. I glanced towards the corridor window where a large blue bottle fly was beating against the glass.

A thought occurred to me. I wondered what it would be like to eavesdrop on the residents. I pretended to leave, made a fuss of pushing back my chair, and opened and closed the glass-panelled door so that the old women would think I had gone.

After a while, a voice spoke. "Who was that?"

No one replied. The clock ticked. I took a step backward into the shadows.

Mary's neighbour leaned towards her. "This place is full of informers," she whispered.

"What?" replied Mary.

"They should do something about it."

"Who should?"

"You were right not to tell him anything."

All their eyes were on Mary. "You're not going to tell anyone are you, Mary?" said her neighbour. "What would be the point? What would anyone gain from it? Nothing that could be of benefit to poor Johnny or you. And it would only cause more harm."

Harm to whom? I wondered.

The room was full of knowing looks and frowns. Another resident rose from her chair, plodded over to Mary and brushed the crumbs from her blouse with a satisfied air.

"Tell them nothing, Mary," she said. "Let your son rest in peace."

Mary waved a hand at her and sighed.

A low rustling noise rose from the room, the sound of more whispering. Mary sat huddled in her armchair, but the others had undergone a transformation. The room was inhabited by old women and their shadows, swaying like underwater plants as they shuffled across the floor, or moved restlessly in their chairs. I kept still. If I tried to slip away now, they would notice me immediately.

Mary's neighbour spoke again. "I haven't forgotten what happened. I think about it all the time.

"Think about what?" asked Mary in a hoarse whisper.

"What they did to poor Johnny."

"They didn't do anything to him."

"A cousin of mine was at Lough Ballinful when it happened. He said the IRA only meant to give him a scare. But Johnny didn't know that. When they held him under the water, he panicked and tried to swim away. The next day, some boys out fishing saw his body floating underwater." She muttered a prayer and a few of the women blessed themselves.

I knew the lough she was talking about. It was full of mud and more than ninety metres deep, too deep for divers, and the bodies of many drownings there had never been recovered. Unless the police suspected foul play, the searches were usually called off after a week or so.

The wrinkles on the old woman's brow deepened.

213

"The boys saw his dead body floating beneath their boat, his face pale as an angel's. They got frightened, rowed back to the shore and ran for their lives. But no one was able to find the body. The police dredged the lough but found nothing. He's still there somewhere, lost in the bottom of the lough."

I hesitated. Was this the ghostly truth I had been searching for? From the depths of the corridor, a small elderly man emerged with a walking-stick and shuffled towards the glass doors. He lifted his head and stared in the exact direction where I was hiding.

It was time to leave, but, before I could turn the door handle, a harsh, correcting voice spoke up.

"It was two nephews of mine who saw the body. But it wasn't Mary's son. It was a young man called Devine from Fintona. The IRA tortured him and held him under the water. But they overdid it and he drowned. The boys thought they saw the reflection of a white swan, but it was his body, moving with the currents. They got the fright of their lives."

Through the glass doors, I watched the care assistant in her trim uniform bending towards a resident. She had only to look through the glass into the shadows to see me. Her uniform slipped lower and I could see the smooth rise of her chest. The old man in the corridor stopped at the door and stared at me with his dark eyes. I could sense his eyes inspect me through the glass, his suspicions magnified by my stillness. The care assistant noticed him and said something. When he turned, I seized the moment and stepped back deeper into the shadows.

Another voice spoke up. "It wasn't a man's body they saw. It was a young woman from Aughnacloy, dressed in a long overcoat the same colour as the mud with her lovely bare feet showing at the bottom. The boys said her face was as still as a wax figure's when it passed under their boat. She was a niece of the Murphy's from Slievemore. She got pregnant and the family thought she'd run away to England with her boyfriend."

Mary's face took on a strange expression, somewhere between indignation and fear. Their stories must have seemed as real as her memories, but she didn't interrupt. This was a group ritual. Even if you didn't participate there was a code to follow.

When I looked again the care assistant was hunkering closer to her patient. I couldn't stay a moment longer, but I was compelled to keep listening. A maternal heat radiated in the room, mournful, agitated, as the stories jumbled on top of each other, closing and vanishing with the same image of a body floating in a bog lake. I was no longer listening to the story of John Harvey. Other disappearances had infiltrated themselves into his story. Scraps and shreds of other tragedies rising vaguely into the light.

"It wasn't a girl they saw," said another old woman. "Two brothers were out swimming together and got into trouble. A fisherman heard their cries and swam to their rescue, but he could only save one of them. The older brother pushed the younger one towards him and then sank quickly. Divers searched for him but never found his body."

"You're wrong," said a voice. "I remember it perfectly. It wasn't a human being at all. It was a donkey that broke out of a field and lost its footing on the rocks. The boys saw its body fall through the air and splash into the water. The only sound it made was the clatter of its hooves on the loose rocks. That's all there is to the story."

It was time to leave, but before I could turn the handle, another old woman spoke up. I looked across and saw that the old man was still watching me like some sort of frowning troll. I realised I had been listening to the old women but had not taken my eyes off the care assistant. He glanced at her and then back at me. I could see from his gaze that he had confirmed his suspicions about me. He raised his stick and tapped the glass.

I rushed forward, opened the door and bumped into the care assistant, who gave a surprised shout. "I'm sorry," I said and hurried down the corridor without looking back.

It was raining as I drove away. Behind me, the nursing home disappeared in the downpour, and the trees and hedgerows seemed to hem in the road more tightly on my homeward journey. Rain drummed upon the roof and against the windscreen. I stared at the vista of ramifying hedges and constant rain, my thoughts groping for an outlet.

John Harvey had hidden with his mother in a farmhouse overlooking miles of windswept bog. He had never been able to leave that place. He had stayed at his mother's side rather than take his chances with a new life in Scotland. He never had a family of his own. He had remained a son of Diseart's thin soil, like generations of his ancestors before him.

I no longer felt a primitive fear over his disappearance, the dread that a human being might be wiped completely from the face of the earth. Harvey had no grave, but at least he had a homeland to which he would always belong and through which his drowned ghost travelled endlessly along paths covered in drifting leaves. The same hidden paths I had followed, circuitous, intricate paths where the living and the dead met and shared their secrets, where everything was still happening, distinct and radiant, where my grandfather roamed as an eleven-year-old boy and I could still follow the fluttering of his handkerchief as though I were following Harvey, picking up clues and obscure facts, linking them together and transforming them into a story.

Perhaps the bullet Harvey had pushed into my hands on the morning of the hijacking had been the seed of a story he had wanted me to write, this story of betrayal and belonging that I still didn't fully understand, but which I was obliged to somehow finish because it was my story, and the story of my grandfather and my parents, told through the imagination and without fear. And now that I had this landscape of invisible paths and silenced stones throbbing in my mind like a fever, the ending was finally in sight.

1982

Alice stood at the seed counter in Woolworth's garden section, examining the varieties of peas. Through a crack in her awareness, John Harvey sneaked into view, his burly figure and earthy hands, the same figure that had haunted so many moments of her day since the hijacking. She looked across and saw that this time it really was him, further along the shelves, peering at packets of cabbage seeds. She tried not to behave differently; her anger had receded, especially since the news of the SAS ambush that had killed his comrades, but her caution remained.

She wondered had he noticed her. He hung on the fringes of her field of vision, rummaging through the rows of packets, a slight smile on his face as though he was daydreaming. It was the last place she expected to see a man like him. She had assumed he was on the run, an exile over the border in the Republic of Ireland, moving furtively from safe-house to safe-house with no time to dream of the future. But there he was, dressed in a woolly jumper with a little smile on his face, planning next year's garden, looking forward to the fruits of belonging, of being rooted in the land, enjoying the daydreams of future vegetable patches and flower beds. Clearly, he didn't consider himself a dangerous killer or a fugitive.

He looked up and across. She felt his eyes study her, gauging her reaction. She hesitated, wondering did she still have the strength to confront him, but before she could decide what to say, he spoke.

"Here we are, Alice. The two of us picking seeds for our gardens."

She looked up and was startled by the sincerity in his gaze, as though he genuinely believed this chance encounter might heal the wounds he had inflicted. She frowned and put her seed packets back onto the racks. How could he have the nerve to talk to her like that? With the same over-familiarity he showed on the morning he had walked into her home with his IRA gang. His manner irritated her. How galling to think he had included her and her family in the act of killing a policeman, and now he was adding this chance meeting to the conspiracy. She searched his face and wondered had he spoken out of irony.

But he was not wearing his balaclava today. His thick fingers were clutching packets of flower and vegetable seeds. He could no longer pretend to be someone else or act as though he would never do what he had already done. His eyes acknowledged their shared secret. She kept her emotions under control. Despite everything, she was calm. Nevertheless, the image of him with a mask and a gun in her living-room wasn't easy to shake off. What had possessed him to do such a thing to another human being, to ruin a policeman's family and the lives of his children? She remembered what she had planned to say to him, but she stopped herself and said nothing.

His presence at the seed counter gave her a new perspective on the past six months, a new sensitivity to their destinies and sense of belonging. She went back to rummaging through the seed packets and was peripherally aware of his growing unease, his boots shuffling on the supermarket floor, his heavy breathing. She repeated his words in her mind and this time understood them better.

"Here we are, Alice, the two of us picking seeds for our gardens."

She grasped the appeal to an amnesty in his words, an

219

absolution of what had happened between their families. Ever since the SAS ambush, a strange mood had settled over Diseart, a muteness tied up with suspicion and fear of betrayal, the same mood that filled her now, stiffening her face like a mask.

Here we are, Alice, the two of us picking seeds for our gardens.

His words created a bond between them, a closeness, upon the solid ground of gardening, sowing and planting seeds. He was just a cousin buying seeds with hope, who wanted to plant and grow something and leave some trace of himself behind. But he had sneaked like an enemy into her home. His violent act had cast a shadow over her family, made the police and security forces look more closely at them, and no one wanted to be looked at in that way when suspicion and betrayal permeated everything. His comrades were dead and there was something unbearable about the steadiness of his gaze, frightening because he was a marked man perched before an abyss. His fall was about to come and here he was, rummaging through racks of seeds for next year's plants, like a ghost longing to take root in the earth.

Here we are, Alice, the two of us picking seeds for our gardens.

But seeds needed time. A great deal of the truth had yet to be told. Some of it lay in the previous six months and some further back in the past, and the truth needed time, too. The story of what had happened would never be forced into existence by a detective or a judge. For now, the story was just a cluster of meetings, a series of cards turned over one by one, her father and his bloody handkerchief, the hijacking, the SAS ambush, and now this chance encounter at the seed shelves. She understood the hidden harmony in Harvey's words. The two of them were the only people left who could tell the story in its entirety.

She looked up and met his eyes, the same glittering eyes that had been haunting her nights for months.

"Are we meant to ignore each other from now on?" he asked, the faint smile still on his lips.

Was he trying to win her over? "I suppose we will," she replied. "For as long as it takes."

"Alright. But I'm still your cousin, Alice. The same John Harvey who used to push you up Paddy's lane in a wheelbarrow."

"Maybe you are and maybe you're not. It doesn't matter who we were back then."

"You could be right."

"I wanted to see you," she said. "I've been looking out for you."

"I don't go out much these days." He lowered his head.

Her hands shook slightly. "I've kept something for you." Her hands shook some more as she reached into her handbag and found the object, still wrapped in a sweetie wrapper. It took some effort, but she lifted it out and handed it to him.

He appeared confused, smiled, looked at the object, felt it with his fingers and frowned. He opened the wrapper slightly and gave her a sudden, surprised stare, his fingers trembling.

Nestled in the wrapper was the bullet he had given her son, the same gift passed on from person to person, from generation to generation, from Donaghy to her grandfather, from the IRA to her son, the same pain handed on and filling lives with trouble.

Harvey's eyes filled with a dark premonition. She had reminded him of the fate that lay in store for him. Her skin prickled and she felt a stab of pity. She could see the fear of death in his eyes. His life, as he knew it, was almost over and all his chances of being the man he truly wanted to be were fading. He would always be remembered as the man who had stepped into his cousin's house with a mask and a gun and then killed a policeman. The person who had dodged an SAS ambush that killed his comrades. A person tainted with violence and betrayal.

Without comment, he went back to the rows of seeds, picked up individual packets, rejected them, going on with his search. She turned and walked towards the supermarket exit. At the threshold, she turned and saw his burly figure still standing there, facing the seed shelves, solemn and still. She left the supermarket and walked down the street. A foot patrol of soldiers was waving guns and checking the parked cars. She pulled her coat collars around her neck, but the wind did not blow as hard and it no longer felt as cold.

*****

Acknowledgements

I'd like to thank my literary agent, Paul Feldstein, for his unwavering support and patience over the past dozen or so years, and also the assistance of the Arts Council of Northern Ireland, who have played a valuable role in encouraging my writing career.

Printed in Great Britain
by Amazon

85212856R00130